Dedalus Original Fiction in Paperback

Time of the Beast

Geoff Smith was born in London and educated in Surrey.
He worked in travel, then wrote and performed for theatre,
television and radio before starting his own business. He is
also a qualified psychotherapist.

Time of the Beast is the result of his longstanding interest in
Anglo-Saxon history and literature, along with a fondness
for classic horror stories.

D1146424

Geoff Smith

TIME
OF THE
BEAST

Dedalus

Supported using public funding by
**ARTS COUNCIL
ENGLAND**

Published in the UK by Dedalus Limited,
24-26, St Judith's Lane, Sawtry, Cambs, PE28 5XE
email: info@dedalusbooks.com
www.dedalusbooks.com

ISBN printed book 978 1 909232 36 5
ISBN ebook 978 1 909232 96 9

Dedalus is distributed in the USA & Canada by SCB Distributors,
15608 South New Century Drive, Gardena, CA 90248
email: info@scbdistributors.com   web: www.scbdistributors.com

Dedalus is distributed in Australia by Peribo Pty Ltd.
58, Beaumont Road, Mount Kuring-gai, N.S.W. 2080
email: info@peribo.com.au

First published by Dedalus in 2014
Time of the Beast copyright © Geoff Smith 2014

The right of Geoff Smith to be identified as the author of this work has been
asserted by him in accordance with the Copyright, Designs and Patents Act,
1988.

Printed in Finland by Bookwell
Typeset by Marie Lane

A C.I.P. listing for this book is available on request.

Now Grendel, with the wrath of God on his back, came out of the moors and the mist-ridden fells...

Beowulf

Then in the stillness of the night it happened suddenly that there came great hosts of the accursed spirits, and they filled all the house with their coming; and they poured in on every side, from above and from beneath, and everywhere. They were in countenance horrible, and they had great heads, and a long neck, and lean visage; they were filthy and squalid in their beards; and they had rough ears, and distorted face, and fierce eyes and foul mouths; and their teeth were like horses' tusks; and their throats were filled with flame, and they were grating in their voice; they had crooked shanks and knees big and great behind, and distorted toes, and shrieked hoarsely with their voices; and they came with such immoderate noises and immense horror, that it seemed to him that all between heaven and earth resounded with their dreadful cries.

From *The Life of St. Guthlac, Hermit of Crowland*, by Felix of Crowland.

Translated by Charles Wycliffe Goodwin.

Chapter One

Greetings, traveller. You may approach. The night is cold, but my fire is warm and it holds the darkness at bay. Come, you may see that I am an old man who means harm to no one. I will be glad of your company. Settle yourself, eat and drink if you will; find companionship and respite from your journey. My own journey? It is nearly over – in every sense. As I sit here I contemplate the darkness as it stretches before me. I see how the night lives, stirred into motion by the leaping flames until the shadows appear to creep and circle about us like spirits that prowl at the gateway to another world. It brings to my mind images from long ago – a time when I wandered deep into the Otherworld on an expedition whose memory seems to me now like a mad and terrible dream.

You wish to know my story? But you will have guessed by now that it is not a comforting tale. Yet it may serve to instruct you, or at least divert you until the morning comes. Very well. Let us look together deep into the shadows which enclose us, and hope that chaos may come to take on the semblance of order.

It was in the year six hundred and sixty-six of our Christian

Age that I, Athwold, a monk, was given leave by my abbot to depart the monastery in the kingdom of East Anglia which had been my home for eleven years, to become at the age of twenty-five a hermit in the great marshland of the Fens. If you have never journeyed in the Fenlands – and I doubt that many ever find cause to do so – it is difficult for me to convey adequately in words just what a forbidding territory that dismal place is. A grim and desolate wasteland of dense high grasses and rushes, a perilous labyrinth with creeping fogs that will rise in a moment to close upon the unwary traveller, leaving him to stumble blind and lost through twisting, treacherous pathways amongst black quagmires and sucking pits that will pull him in an instant to his death. There are foul and stagnant pools, streams and rivulets which abound with leeches, stinging flies and all manner of vile parasites; and worst of all are the foul-smelling miasmas which float above the tainted waters, creating a poisonous atmosphere of unremitting gloom in a land of misty and near-perpetual twilight. The very gateway to Hell. In short, the ideal place for a religious retreat.

The Fenland is vast, almost a murky kingdom in itself, and its depths stand uncharted and ungoverned beyond every law of man; the natural refuge of outcasts, outlaws and other still worse things of ill omen. I journeyed there first upon a bright, sharp spring day to a settlement situated on the flat grasslands close to the western edge of the Fens, accompanied by my guide, a native man named Wecca, whose services had been arranged for me by the local Christian mission. No man knew these lands better than he, Wecca assured me, and he would lead me deep into the marshes to find some suitable place of refuge for me. He was a man approaching middle-life – I judged him to be about thirty – and he told me how in his youth he had gone to fight for the Christian King Anna of the

East Angles in his war against old King Penda, the last pagan ruler of the kingdom of Mercia. Wecca was a handsome man with clear, pale blue eyes which beamed out from the wild tangle of his flaxen hair and beard. He looked to me like an angel peeping through a bush.

The village we approached was a typical farmstead, surrounded by pastures full of grazing cattle and sheep. It was clearly a prosperous place with many timber structures of varying sizes, their thatched roofs visible from miles away as they poured clouds of grey smoke into the open sky. The whole village was encircled by a protective trench and a palisade. I would spend the night at this outpost, then tomorrow begin my search in the Fens for the place of my seclusion.

As we drew near, Wecca blew on the brass horn that hung from his neck to signal our presence. The men of the village soon emerged in a crowd to greet us, clad in their brightly coloured woollen tunics and dark trousers, some with long cloaks held at the shoulders by ornate bronze clasps. They carried spears, but only from habit, it seemed, for our arrival was expected and their faces were welcoming and friendly. These men were of the tribe called Gyrwas, or fen-men, a famously independent people, for they knew themselves to inhabit the fringes of a land where no king might assert his rule effectively. But it encouraged me to see that a roughly made wooden shrine to the Cross stood at the gateway to their village. The men treated me with respect and reverence, regarding me as a kind of holy man. And, I learned later, a brave one.

I was taken to a guest hut, a place quite comfortable by the standards of a monk accustomed to only a bare cell. I had learned to distrust comfort, but I consoled myself with the thought that soon I would know little enough of it. The village outside was intolerably noisy with the grunting of pigs, the clucking of hens and the incessant screaming of small children. It would be almost impossible, I concluded sadly, for a man to clear his thoughts sufficiently to reflect upon God in a place of so many distractions. And the stink was abominable.

That evening I was led along a muddy pathway to the village beer hall, where a feast had been prepared in my honour. I would not have wished for such a thing, but I knew that hospitality was regarded as a tradition and a duty by these people, even when it meant that all might starve for it later.

When I entered their hall – dark, smoky and filled with the warm smell of cooking meat – the men rose from their benches out of respect, and were not seated again until I was escorted into the chair of the high guest. This made me feel uneasy. I was not a bishop or a priest, or any Church dignitary, only a humble monk passing through; and in those days I was much concerned with humility, or at least the outward appearance of it. Nevertheless it gratified me that these men honoured the Church through me. They were God-fearing people. So it seemed.

Soon the great iron cooking pot which stood on high trestles above the fire was lowered to the ground by dark-haired Celts, slaves in rough tunics and crude metal neck-bands to denote their lack of status. They carried the food to us on huge wooden platters: venison and fowl, along with sausages and blood puddings, and loaves of freshly baked bread. And there was also much strong drink: the milder ale and the more potent beer. I drank only a cup of the ale mixed with water and ate mostly bread with an occasional mouthful of chicken, for my order prohibited the consumption of red meat. To find the right balance was important, for I must demonstrate my appreciation while appearing to remain appropriately abstemious. Only the village men were present at this banquet: perhaps they considered women unsuitable company for a celibate monk. I thought this view most proper. When we had finished eating, we were subjected to the verses of a *scop* – a bard who plucked with indifferent skill upon a lyre, while reciting some interminable heathen tale about a hero who battled with a monster in a marsh.

As the evening went on, the men about me became increasingly drunk – to my growing concern and disapproval – until at last it seemed that I was the only sober man left in the hall. But with drunkenness they became more bold and outspoken, and some of the distance between us appeared to diminish – until then they had seemed like shy, awkward children who did not know quite how to address me. Yet now they began to overcome their timidity and questioned me openly about my intention to live as a recluse in the Fens. As light from the torches which hung from iron sconces on the flame-blackened walls bathed their bushy, bemused faces, it was clear that the notion was wholly inexplicable to them, even on the part of an inscrutable holy man.

'Do you know?' they whispered, crowding about me as their eyes grew wide and their faces darkened. 'There are bad things. Out in the fen. Bad things in the darkness. In the night.'

Of course it was clear to me that the Fens must contain a multitude of natural perils. This must be obvious to anyone, and it was what made those sparsely populated wastelands the place of solitude I sought. But the manner of these men seemed at once guarded and fearful in a way that did not suggest a concern for natural things. To my further questions they did not reply directly, but merely cast ominous glances at each other and mumbled evasively as they shook their heads. None were by now sober enough to remember to make the sign of the Cross while they muttered darkly, if only as a gesture to please me.

I nodded at them gravely as I began to understand. They would not speak openly of their credulous terrors, fearing a primitive superstition that they might be heard by something outside – something grim and malevolent – and give it power over them. 'To speak of the Devil is to bid him come', as the saying goes.

I felt sudden anger towards these simple-minded men, and in my heart I began to despise them, although I told myself that my feelings were rather those of pity. In my younger days I had turned from the old pagan beliefs of my ancestors to embrace with zeal the new Faith of Christ. I knew with all the certainty of youth that our Church was the shining beacon of the one true God, which would lead men out of darkness and into the light. It would unite the petty scattered kingdoms of Britain under a single discipline and creed, even to make us one with our brother-lands in Europe. I never doubted that the Church would succeed in its holy mission to civilise our world, to foster learning and bring wisdom, to broker peace and lead us beyond the tribal rivalries and wars that so often lay waste to our fragmented lands. It was only a question of how long these things would take. And I had every reason to be optimistic. For I had seen in my own short lifetime the remarkable triumphs of the Church over the dark ways of paganism; and by the time I went into the Fenlands every Angle and Saxon kingdom of Britain, save for the backward South Saxons and the barbarous inhabitants of the island called Wight, had been won over to Christ. Kingdom by kingdom, region by region, we had taken these lands, replacing heathen idols with Christian ideals.

But that night among the Gyrwas I was filled with a sense of weary despair. These people called themselves Christians, but it was quite clear to me they were in truth barely reformed savages who still inhabited a world of squalid primitive superstitions and were ready at any sign of adversity to scurry back to the worship of devils and so damn their souls. Was it for this that the Church had fought so hard to convert them? The preachers from the local mission had clearly been remiss in their duties, for it seemed a miserable achievement. I saw now that these men were misguided and ignorant, and their lives were governed by irrational fears. Yet I knew I walked in the light while they stumbled in darkness, and I understood that it was by the conquest of fear that a true Christian set himself apart from other men.

I took a deep breath as I reflected on my position. For I had not come here with any intent to be a preacher or missionary. I sought and longed only for solitude. The truth was that I approached a great crisis in my own life, and while I was not yet certain of its true nature, I had long sensed its coming. Alone upon the fen, I made ready to do battle with my gathering demons. But it seemed to me then to be something more than just coincidence that I stood in that hall, at that moment, facing those men who were so close to the pit of eternal damnation. I felt with certainty that I was the Lord's appointed messenger here, the agent of His Church, sent to correct these people in their ways of error. I must lay aside for the moment my monk's humility.

'Take heed, you men!' I called out. 'Do you think the Devil sends his minions to prowl in the darkness like your imaginary hobgoblins, to attack men without cause? I tell you this is not so. The Devil seeks not the flesh but the soul of a man. It is sin, and sin alone, that makes us vulnerable to the Unholy One.' I paused, gazing at them fiercely. Then in my anger I tutted loudly and wagged a reproachful finger at them. They stood, all rooted to the spot, their drunken eyes at once bulging and fearful. This was good, for I must terrify them more than all their monsters in the mist. 'The Devil is ever watchful and ready to tempt men into sin,' I cried, 'for it is by sin that Satan prospers. And one day – *perhaps one day soon* – if the weight of man's sin upon the world grows to become so great that God turns His face from us, then the Devil will be freed from Hell to fall on this world and destroy it, to burn it to ashes in a *great burst of fire!*' I flung my arms up wildly as I glowered at them, eliciting gasps and groans of dismay.

I was not certain how much they grasped of this; not even sure to what extent they understood the very concept of sin. It mattered only that they were impressed by my severity. They were simple people. In fact I thought them rather stupid. So I decided to make my message more direct.

'Thus I say to you, do not fear the darkness without, but tremble and look to the darkness within, for there lies the Devil's hunting ground. But the man who overcomes his sinful ways need have no fear of the Devil and his snares.' I threw up my head. 'I will go out into the wilderness and show you there is nothing there for a righteous man to fear. I will set you a good Christian example.' And I concluded with some lines from one of the psalms, which seemed to me most apt:

> Patiently I awaited the Lord;
> He turned to me and heard my cry.
> He raised me up from the lonely pit,
> From out of the miry bog,
> And set my feet upon stone,
> To make my steps secure.

Then, much pleased with my actions, I bowed my head to

them and walked to the doors, where I turned and said:

'Now I must rest. Goodnight to you, my friends. And thank you for a most convivial evening.'

Then I went off to my bed.

That night I was afflicted by the visitation of a terrible dream. I found myself wandering inside a dark woodland, lit only by moonbeams which faintly penetrated, here and there, the thick canopy of leaves and branches above, dappling the forest floor with small patches of faint silvery light. Somewhere nearby a soft voice called my name, and I began to follow it, stumbling over uneven ground, through bushes and around trees. Occasionally I caught the merest glimpse of a figure ahead that ran and weaved through the night before me, taunting my senses as I sought to fix my eyes upon it. It was like watching a fish darting in a stream. I was racing hard to catch this fleeting form – for what reason I could not tell – yet however much I strove to increase my pace, I was not able to close the distance between us. But as I went on, I slowly gained the impression of a girl, and my mind was filled with the image of long swishing hair, of firm breasts and slim bare legs beneath a short gown so delicate and flimsy it might have been woven from a spider's web. Then she laughed, a tinkling, intoxicating sound as she raced onward through the wood like a skittish wild creature.

All at once I emerged into what was like a dark glade, but as I ran my foot struck against some small prominence in the earth, and I stumbled and fell, to find myself lying face-down in the high grass. But I did not rest upon the hard ground, for I became suddenly aware, with a sense of pure alarm, that I was sprawled on top of another body, which lay on its back and looked up at me from amidst shadows which entirely concealed its face. I reached out my hands, attempting to raise myself up, but as I did so my fingers pressed down onto warm, yielding flesh, and there came from under me another peal of that soft, sensuous laughter. I tried to pull my hands away, yet they felt leaden and beyond my control; and then they started to move as if by their own will, as I lay with all the helplessness of the dreamer, unable to break free from the forbidden sensations which were unfolding beneath me. I attempted to speak, but no words would come as my breath rose and fell in feverish gulps. I could hear the deep steady breathing of the other body, as inch by inch my hands crept upward over its firm rounded contours, and came finally to rest on the fleshy mounds of its breasts.

Now the form shuddered slightly, and gave a soft sigh, seeming to take exquisite pleasure from this. And I was becoming lost as I sank down into its warm embrace. Until abruptly, in a single movement, the figure sat rigidly upright, bringing its face close to mine, so that finally I could see it clearly in the moonlight. It was the face of my own mother, dead for three years, gazing sternly back at me, her mouth fixed into a crooked rictus.

I awoke with a cry, dry-mouthed and drenched in sweat. It was still dark, and I reached out with a shaking hand to scoop a cup of water from the bucket beside my bed, drinking half of it, then splashing what remained over my face.

The dream had been an alarming one, more so because it seemed vaguely to me in those initial moments of awakening that this was not the first time I had experienced a dream of this kind. But as I became more fully awake this feeling seemed to drift away, and I rose up, then fell to my knees and prayed there fervently until the first light of day crept beneath the door to my hut and the noises from the stirring village began to rise all about me.

By the time I finished my prayers my mind felt less troubled, for I had begun to make sense of my dream. I saw that while its grossly sensual aspects had been deeply disturbing and nightmarish, I had been delivered from these horrors by the salutary image of my dead mother, rising up to drive all such impure urges away. Perhaps, I reflected, these things had been the symbols of a higher truth: that the Devil had sent a succubus to tempt me, and that my own mother had represented the Holy Mother, our blessed Virgin herself, who had interceded on my behalf. These thoughts brought me much comfort and reassurance as I went out into the daylight with a renewed sense of resolution. The dream felt like a happy omen and a sign that Heaven itself smiled upon my intentions, while the Devil cursed me for them.

Chapter Two

Soon I departed from the village with Wecca. It was my good fortune that the day was dry and mild, and the sky was clear. We went on foot, for this was the only practical way to journey through the marshes, although some parts of the Fens are accessible by boat along the rivers and wider streams. On the way I noticed in the distance the crumbling ruins of an ancient Roman fort, and I asked Wecca whether it was true, as I had once been told, that centuries ago the old Romans had attempted to drain parts of the Fens and turn them into arable land, although to truly tame any part of those intractable swamps had proved to be finally beyond the powers of even the Romans. Wecca shrugged, and frowned, then replied in his mangled dialect:

'It is maybe true. There are some few ruin of old Romans hereabouts. I do not know the purpose they serve, long time ago. My people, we stay away from these places, Brother. Built from stone by dark magic and given over to Roman devils. Evil spirits live in them still.' He stopped himself abruptly and looked at me uneasily. No doubt he recalled the rebuke I had given to the village men the previous night for their idle superstitions.

'There is nothing to fear in those old buildings, Wecca,' I told him, 'except for lumps of stone that may fall onto your head. The Romans merely possessed the knowledge to build with stone, which our people lack.'

We made good progress at first, and it was only a short time before the open marshlands stretched before us, and the ground grew more boggy and wet. We trudged onward, our feet sinking into soft mud as we waded through shallow pools of dark sludge and fetid weeds, our passage becoming ever harder and slower. High grass and reeds rose to envelop us, while our surroundings grew more bleak and inhospitable. Wecca went before me, finding the safe paths and hacking a way through the thicker patches of vegetation with his *seax* – his long knife. Our destination was an island deep in the marshes in the territory known as the Crowland. Wecca informed me that this island was habitable and said others had attempted to settle there in the distant past, but now it was entirely deserted.

The sun was at its height, and we had travelled half the day without stopping when we came to some woodlands that gradually inclined above the sunken marshes, and as we entered them I felt the ground become firmer. These wooded knolls stretched far before us and were the only landmarks for miles around. I turned quickly to survey the terrain behind, which we had traversed that day: a vast expanse of wild, grey and silent monotony. It was as dark and despairing as anything I might have hoped for.

At length we came to a winding stream, and we followed this until we reached a place where numerous other pools and rivulets converged, to create within their midst a collection of small wooded islands, many of them half-concealed by the dense undergrowth. One of these was our destination. It was a good place, Wecca assured me; the water was clean, and there were fish to add to my diet, should I care to catch them. But I had taken a vow that I would allow myself no such luxury, but would be sustained upon plain bread alone. Wecca led me to a place on the bank of a wide stream and told me that this was the shallowest point where we might cross over to the island. Then he threw down his cloak, pulled off his muddy boots, stripped himself of his tunic and trousers, and carrying only his knife he strode quite naked, apart from his array of necklaces and arm rings, into the stream. I stood and watched him wade across, and saw that at the deepest point the water came up to his neck. Then he emerged and clambered through the mud on the opposite bank, and turned to face me.

'Come,' he called to me. 'It is safe. But you should take off clothes. It will not be good to walk in them muddy and wet. It will make sores come.'

I could not deny this suggestion was sensible, so hurriedly I undressed, laying my boots and robe on the bank, but then rolling up my cloak and taking it with me, holding it above my head to keep it dry as I entered the stream. As I waded in deeper I gave an involuntary gasp, as instantly the soft current of the chill water brought to my body a cold sensual thrill, a sudden and intense awareness of my entire physical self. And for the moment I became frozen, quite unable to move as the sensation seemed to overwhelm me. Then I stirred myself and went onward to the far bank. As I rose from the water I was at once aware of Wecca, standing nearby and gazing at my body with an undisguised interest. Feeling awkward I turned away, brushing off the clinging drops of water as I unrolled my cloak, then threw it on and wrapped it about me. I turned back to Wecca. He was still staring at me, now in what seemed like surprise, as if my wish to cover myself were only another example of my incomprehensible eccentricity. These people had no sense of bodily shame whatsoever – another legacy of their primitive pagan habits. It was a thing in which the Church still strove to educate them. After a few moments he said quietly:

'It is good to see…'

'What is?' I said, a little astonished.

'That a holy man,' he pointed to me and smiled, then raised his hands to indicate his own nakedness, 'is made like other men.' He seemed somehow pleased by this.

'But a monk is a man,' I told him in exasperation, for his expression suggested that until now he had not been wholly convinced of this. I could only wonder vaguely what he might have expected.

'Good to see,' he repeated with a nod, then added firmly: 'We are goodly men.' I could make nothing of this. Then he said to reassure me: 'This is a fine island. It never floods. Come, I will show you.'

He turned to lead me, although this hardly seemed necessary, since most of the island was visible from where we stood. I followed him for a brief while, concentrating mostly on averting my eyes, as I began to find that his careless nudity was disconcerting me. At last I said to him:

'Thank you, Wecca. You may go back now and wait for me across the stream. I would like to look around on my own.'

He nodded without offence and strolled away. I began to wander about, inspecting this potential refuge which was in fact just a grassy wooded hillock surrounded by water.

That day, as I have said, was mild and pleasant, and even the ever-present Fenland mist was but the merest wisps of vapour on the waters, while soft sunlight shone down to warm my face. But even this could not disguise what a truly forlorn and barren place this was. A life spent here could only be one of damp, cold and squalid privation. It was exactly what I sought.

In the middle of the island, at its highest point, I discovered an ancient tumulus, a tall solid burial mound of earth, covered with heavy stones which had clearly been brought here from somewhere beyond the marshes. At its base on one side, the large rocks had at some time been torn away, and an attempt had been made to excavate down inside the structure in a search for treasures and grave goods buried alongside the bones of whoever lay there. I was most surprised to find this rugged tribute to the dead in such a remote place, the only sign that there had ever been any human habitation here. Clearly any settlers had long ago abandoned this island, unable to eke out a living here. But this did not concern me, for their needs had not been the same as mine. Yet it did occur to me that the tumulus might be useful. It could serve as a solid foundation, to support the shelter I must build for myself. Now I must return to my monastery to bid farewell to my brothers and come back with building materials and men to assist me. Then I would be entirely alone.

Finally I returned to cross back over the stream and pulled off my cloak as I strode into the water. But this time I allowed myself no moment of pause, no brief sensation of indulgence or pleasure. I hurried across to the opposite bank, snatching up my clothes and pulling them on while I was still wet. Then I went to find Wecca. I discovered him lying on the grass nearby. He was on his back, his arms stretched up to rest his head in his hands. He was still naked, drying his body in the faint sunlight; and as I drew near I saw he had fallen into a light sleep. In that moment I felt loath to wake him, for he appeared so tranquil and innocent, this great rough-looking man. As I stood over him, I found I was beginning to stare with a growing fascination at his body, exposed there in the golden glow of the sun. I told myself as I did so that this was to reassure me that there truly were no innate differences between us, as he had supposed there might be. But in fact there were differences, for mine was the thin body of a monk from the scriptorium, and his was a sturdy frame with powerful muscles and old scars visible on his arms and legs, the wages of years of toil and battle.

It had been many years since I last gazed directly upon an unclothed human form, not since my childhood in fact. When I went with other monks from the monastery into the outside world, I would sometimes see people bathing and swimming in ponds and streams, but I had been strictly instructed that it was seemly to turn my eyes from this. Now that I found myself alone, looking secretly upon this uncovered body, I found I was unable to tear my gaze from it. I reflected that my stare was born of innocent admiration for this perfect example of God's creation, this fleshly instrument so ideally fitted for the life it led. But still my eyes lingered with a devouring intimacy upon the small goose-bumps that covered the pale skin in the open air, the broad chest covered in thick hair that rose and fell in a gentle rhythm, and the thin line of down that ran along the middle of the flat torso and was lost amongst the wild growth of curls about the groin.

Suddenly Wecca sighed faintly and stirred a little in his sleep. As he did so I felt a tingling sense of shock, for I saw at once that his organ began to stiffen and rise, becoming tumescent in a few moments. In that instant his eyes opened, and he looked up at me, smiling drowsily. I turned away in alarm and tried to quell the tremble in my voice as I said:

'We are finished here. I have decided this place will

be suitable.'

He stood, and moved before me, his member still half erect, although he did not seem to notice this, or else to care. Then he nodded and said:

'Yes. I tell you this island is best.'

'Thank you, Wecca,' I said. 'Your advice was sound. Now go and get dressed. We should leave.'

'Yes.' He thought for a moment and said, 'We must go while there is still much light.'

Then he turned and pissed copiously into the grass, before going off to put on his clothes. When he returned it seemed his mood had changed, for I saw that his face appeared troubled. He stood in silence and looked at me with apparent nervousness.

'What is it, Wecca?' I asked him. 'What is the matter?'

He approached me, seeming lost for words, then he fell to his knees and grasped at my legs.

'There is much I would tell you,' he cried out in sudden distress. 'But you will be angry at me and call me a bad man. You will call me sinner and curse me.'

At his touch I felt a strange, slightly dizzy sensation as my heart began to pound. I did not like people touching me.

'I will not be angry, Wecca,' I said, my voice faint as my throat grew tight. 'Whatever it is… I promise… I will not.' I reached out to motion him to his feet. He stood for a moment, his wide blue eyes staring into mine, and once more I was struck by his wild beauty. Then without warning he flung himself at me, his arms enfolding me as he swept me to him in a powerful embrace, his cheek pressed to mine. And my strength simply melted away as I stood quivering and powerless, unable to move or think, trapped there in his arms. While I knew in my mind I must try to break free and demand some explanation, my body would not respond and I felt I had no ability to resist him.

'Brother,' he gasped into my ear, and it seemed he struggled to speak. 'You know most men be good and natural men. But other men be not natural men and do not do natural things. But these not natural men are true men. This you must believe.' I heard his words only vaguely, for my body was overcome and I seemed to be sinking into a kind of daze. Then he thrust me backward, grasping my shoulders and holding me at arm's length, restoring to me a little of my senses, before he pulled me close to him again, our eyes meeting as I felt the stirring of his breath and the warmth of his body against me. 'Do you understand what I say?' he urged me, and I looked back at him, still overwhelmed as I attempted to shake my head. He drew closer still, his breath hot on my ear, and spoke in a whisper which made it seem as if he feared some intruder might overhear us in this incredibly remote place. But I did not listen to his words. For it was now I recalled the previous night and the fearful reluctance of the village men to speak openly of their superstitious beliefs. At once I began to understand. Wecca was attempting to warn me against something, and when he said that 'Not natural men are true men' he spoke of his own conviction that the tales of unnatural beings which prowled in the Fens were true.

I stood, my mind simply blank and stunned, barely comprehending what had just happened. I could not believe my own passive response to Wecca's alarming actions, my seeming inability to offer any resistance.

Wecca was still talking, whispering all manner of wild nonsense, encouraged by my failure to react angrily. I was still too immersed in my own state of shock and dismay to listen to him closely, but what he seemed to be telling me was that the remnants and survivors of old and terrible races still inhabited, in isolated pockets, the deepest and darkest reaches of the Fens. He meant that over the centuries the waves of invaders who had flooded into our isles had supplanted, time and again, the earlier inhabitants, who had fled to seek shelter in the most wild and remote regions of the land, to live there in dwindling numbers, practising their primitive magic, growing inbred and deformed until they were no longer like men at all – if indeed they had ever been. I had heard of these superstitions before. The Church called these mythical creatures the *hominem silvestrem* or wild men of the forest. Some credulous folk imagined they were not in fact the fleshly scions of monsters at all, but rather the vengeful ghosts of the monsters themselves. Where the wild men were concerned, many were uncertain where degraded flesh ended and dark spirit began.

I found these delusions interesting, for I believed I understood how they had come about. When, two centuries ago, our own peoples had come to Britain from our Germanic homelands, we had driven back many of the native population – the Celtic Britons – until now they occupied mostly the western parts of the island: the lands of the outsiders, whom we call the *wealas*. But it seemed most likely that some Britons, fleeing subjection or slavery, had retreated into the concealment of these great Fens, and that their descendants might still exist here in small groups and must surely appear to be strange and alien if ever sighted by people like Wecca, who had supposed even monks might be made differently to other men.

Yet I found I could not be angry with Wecca for his foolish beliefs, for it was clear his warning was one of honest concern, and that he had risked my wrath to give it. I simply assured him that a good Christian had nothing to fear from the hearth-side tales of old women. But I thanked him for the basic good sense of his advice, which was never to wander too deeply into the fen, and *never* at night.

But as we trekked back that afternoon through the marshes, my mind was much disturbed. For it was very clear to me that I, a monk and a servant of God who had willingly taken my strict vows of renunciation of the flesh, should not have found myself entranced in the sunlight by the bare skin of a common woodsman, nor overcome by his sudden embrace. And as I gazed at the sturdy form of Wecca, striding in front of me, I found myself at once stricken by a sense of pure anger towards him; and in my heart I cursed him for an ignorant fool and a shameless savage.

Chapter Three

Next I travelled by river up to the north coast of East Anglia, where I discussed with the boatmen there the practical arrangements for transporting men and materials into the Fens. It was not an easy matter, but one that could be managed. I was able to inform the head boatman that one of our revered saints, the blessed St. Dado, had died a glorious martyr's death at a place nearby, many years ago, as a missionary preaching the Faith to the pagans. He told me he knew the story, and what he had heard was that the blessed Dado had gone to preach at the hall of the local lord, where everyone regarded him as a harmless lunatic, until one night, when the warriors in the beer hall were more than usually intoxicated, someone had discovered the drunken Dado attempting to fornicate with a goat. So they all took him out to use him for target practice, and he had died bleating like the object of his desire. That was often the way with such men, he smirked, 'Cross in one hand and cock in the other.' Much angered, I cautioned him for his soul's sake never again to repeat this malicious calumny. Then I concluded my business and set out to return to my monastery.

Some time after my arrival there, I was summoned to

an audience with the abbot, a man named Adelard, in his private study. It was an impressive chamber – unlike the plain dwellings of the other monks – with a shuttered window which faced the setting sun, and walls adorned with shelves full of hide-bound books – an enormous treasure – along with fine wood carvings depicting Biblical scenes. Abbot Adelard was a Frank, who spoke Anglish perfectly, although still with a strong accent, and he greeted me with his customary dignity of manner. He was a man of advanced years, perhaps fifty, but his mild exterior concealed a true fierceness in his devotion to the doctrines of the Church.

'So, Brother Athwold,' he said, as he motioned to me to stand before him. 'You are determined to persist with this matter of yours?'

'I am, Father Abbot,' I replied.

'And the reason for your decision, the troubles and dissatisfactions in your mind, I must presume they remain unresolved?'

'Yes, Father Abbot.'

'I must tell you, Brother,' he said, 'that your longing after a life of seclusion has won you much esteem here in our community. The younger monks especially seem to admire your resolve to commit yourself to an existence of solitary contemplation.' He shrugged. 'And why not? Such sacrifice is an admirable thing. So most men believe.' I was aware now that a discordant note had crept into his voice. 'But I feel compelled to ask myself what would be the condition of the Church if all those who serve in it were to abandon their responsibilities and seek escape from the world? The answer is most clearly that the enterprise of our Holy Church would die. So I say to you, Brother Athwold, look carefully and study closely your own motives in this, and consider if what you are doing is truly a thing of devotion and humility, or really just an act of intransigence and pride.' He paused and looked hard at me, for there was significance in these last words. 'I know your opinion of the Irish matter. Indeed you made it very clear. You made it a source of contention all about you. You, who I once thought to be a man of such loyalty to the Church. But you have seen fit to question the wisdom of your superiors and even of the blessed Augustine himself.'

At that moment Abbot Adelard and I seemed to be returned to our positions of nearly two years before. Back then, the Irish matter had been controversial. My own opinion of it had been outspoken, and unusually at variance with the prevailing view within our Catholic Church.

The matter concerned the long and bitter dispute between two Christian sects – the Celtic Church of Britain and Ireland, and the Catholic Church of Rome. British Celts are of course Christians – though often poor ones – a legacy from the days when Britain was a province of the old Roman Empire. But over two hundred years ago, when the Empire of Rome collapsed in the west, the British and Roman churches were split and separated as pagan barbarians overran much of Europe, and the British Church began to exist independently from the Roman. At that time a British missionary named Patricius took the Christian Faith across the sea to the Irish peoples; as the pagan Angles, Saxons, Jutes and others began their migration into Britain. Later, the now devout Irish Church sent its own Christian missionaries into Britain to begin converting these heathen settlers – the native British refused to do so, for there was constant war between them.

Then, about seventy years ago, Pope Gregory had sent the monk Augustine on his famous mission to Britain, to Kent, the southern kingdom of the Jutes, to win the pagan lands for the Roman Church. So while Irish missionaries won converts among the Picts and Angles of northern Britain, spreading down from their base upon the Island of Hii, or Iona, in the far north, the Roman Catholics established their mission in the south. In time an unseemly rivalry arose. For by now the Roman and Celtic churches had grown far apart in their customs and practices.

The Romans greatly disapproved of the Britons' unorthodoxy, and regarded the whole British Church as merely an upstart and heretical offshoot of their own. But Augustine, who was now archbishop, saw that if the Britons could be persuaded to adopt the Roman ways, then this would greatly add to the authority and prestige of his own Church. He decided that the British Church was a thing ripe to be taken over. But he botched the matter completely. At first he decreed that the British clergy were to be artfully persuaded into becoming Roman Catholics. But when they proved stubborn in their own traditions, Augustine became incensed.

'Who are these Britons,' he thundered, 'to resist and obstruct us? They must be compelled to comply.'

A conference was arranged between Augustine and the religious leaders among the Britons. Church records exonerate Augustine from all blame for its failure, but it is easy to read between the lines. Augustine greeted the British clergymen without respect and glowered at them menacingly throughout the debate, seeking only to intimidate them. The Britons became antagonised, and when Augustine saw they would not be bullied into obedience, he flew into a rage and cursed them to their faces, threatening damnation and destruction on them before storming out. And so an opportunity was missed, and the two churches remained divided and unreconciled. I always felt that Augustine's behaviour in this matter was quite shocking.

Then came the Irish missionaries, bringing their own version of Celtic Christianity. When I was a child, my family and I were converted to the Faith by Irish preachers. I learned to admire and respect them greatly. I particularly remember a monk named Conchobar. He was an awesome-looking man, tall and rugged, his tonsure cut in the peculiar Irish way – the 'old way' as he called it – with the front and top of his head wholly shaved, leaving only his long and unruly locks at the back. He never washed or cut his beard, and he wore a filthy robe which he never took off, although it was so worn and ragged it tended to expose every part of him. His fasts would last for weeks, while he would sometimes sit on a rock and meditate for days. In winter he would wade into the river and stand for hours in the freezing water. *'It is colder in Hell!'* he would cry. And he was fervent in his condemnation of sin – 'the mortal enemy to be excised from men'. I thought him a remarkable man.

When I decided to receive the tonsure, I reflected long and hard over which church I should join. Finally I chose the Roman, as the first and universal Church. I think I was also intimidated by what I saw of the harshness of the lives of the Irish monks. And for years I remained content in my choice.

The antipathy between the churches continued to grow over the years. In my monastery the Irish were derided as idiotic and filthy creatures. Irish jokes abounded. Yet I knew their beliefs were strong and sincere, and I was angered by this discord over matters of mere form between fellow Christians. I admired the devout Irish ways of poverty and humility – qualities for which our high Roman churchmen were certainly not renowned. Then news came that the matter was to be settled finally. There was to be a synod held in the north – the stronghold of the Irish – at a monastery in a place called the

Bay of the Light, where King Oswy of Northumbria would decide between the two churches, and declare whose rituals and doctrines should in future be adopted in his kingdom. No one could fail to understand the significance of this. It was an open bid by the Roman Catholics to become predominant within the Irish heartlands.

My monastery was filled with excited debate over this matter. Abbot Adelard and other monks of high rank, spoke of it as the final battle in a great and glorious war. I grew angry, and told my brother monks that the synod was set as a trap, for the Irish advocates – doubtless honest and plain-spoken men – would never sway a king in council like the smooth and polished politicians of our Church. Before I was aware of it, I had become a dissenting voice. And the other monks always seemed keen to encourage me in my outspokenness. Then one day in discussion, I remarked that this whole matter might have been settled years before with peaceful compromise had it not been for the *intransigence and pride* of Augustine.

Later that day I was summoned into the presence of Abbot Adelard. He gazed at me for a time without speaking, but his expression was enough to tell me my transgression had been grave.

'Blasphemy!' he spat at last.

'Father Abbot?' I looked at him with astonishment. Perhaps my words had been hasty and imprudent, but blasphemy? They were hardly that.

'Do you think, Brother Athwold, that any word spoken in this monastery remains unknown to me?' He glared at me savagely. Truly he was in a fury, barely able to control himself. 'And I say your words were a blasphemy. That a mere and supposedly humble monk should speak so of our blessed Augustine – that holy man! – the founder of our Church in

35

these lands. That a member of this community…' he stopped, apparently speechless, shaking his head in disbelief.

'I am truly sorry, Father Abbot,' I said, as his rage began to frighten me.

'I will not tolerate such insolence!' he shouted suddenly, his face growing red. 'I am amazed, Brother, that you would speak openly to criticise our Church in defence of that deplorable nest of Irish heretics.'

'My apologies again, Father,' I murmured, hanging my head. 'I was only distressed to see such divisions among Christians…'

'*Christians!*' he hissed. 'They cannot be dignified by the name – they do not keep Easter at its proper time or practice the sacraments as we do; they even consult with their local people in matters of religious custom, if such a thing can be believed. And then there is the abomination of their tonsure. They are barely better than pagans. Hardly like us in any way, for their customs are a foul and loathsome parody of our own.'

'They are godly men, Father Abbot,' I objected, shocked by the force of his contempt, and finding that slowly my fear was turning into anger. 'I believe the differences between us are only small matters…'

'Ah!' he said with a scowl. 'I suspect now I have nurtured a serpent inside my Eden. Let me instruct you, Brother. Let me tell you about your "godly men". Time and again, we of the true Church have sought to persuade them from their ways of transgression. We send to them rulings from our archbishop, and even directives from his Holiness, in our efforts to correct them. We have requested they supply specifics of their rituals and practices, to show them where they err, and demanded reports of their attempts to convert the pagans – facts, figures and details. But they simply refuse to respond. They are truly monsters!'

'But, Father Abbot,' I said mildly, 'they are merely not familiar with our Roman ways. Remember that Ireland was never a part of the old Empire. The Irish simply do not understand the concept of a central authority. They are concerned with the business of saving souls, rather than in compiling records about it. Surely we cannot despise them for this?'

'Monsters, wicked monsters, to defy us so!' he growled under his breath. 'They follow no true doctrine but act according to their own interpretations. This cannot be tolerated. You should understand that it is our skills of organisation and orderly administration which have been the greatest weapon in our conquest and control of these lands and their ignorant illiterate natives. For nothing frightens and browbeats them more that the writings on a document.' He seemed to forget, or ignore, the fact that I was a native. Then he said softly, as if to himself: 'Ah, yes. It is our talent for these things that in the end will make them all into our bondsmen.' Then his voice rose again in anger. 'But do not suppose for all our successes that our victory is assured. Remember our past reverses among the Northumbrians, and the East Saxons, and others, that demonstrate clearly how fragile our hold upon these chaotic lands remains. The pagans retreat, yet they still have the power to corrupt. So must all Christians remain *united,* to speak with one voice. In this house mine is the voice of the Church, and it is your place only to accept and obey. Understand me, Brother Athwold. My authority here is absolute, and I will endure no words of dissent. Reflect upon your *maleficium* – your shameful misdeed – and know that if you offend again it will be my place to determine your fate.'

I bowed my head to him in meek and abject submission. But even as I did so there was born in my heart the secret spark of defiance and fury whose flame was to grow and consume me. I saw then that Adelard – the voice of the Church – cared nothing for honesty or conscience, but solely for his own authority, and my docile surrender and conformity. He concerned himself only with the politics of the world, and sought to bully and intimidate me just as Augustine had with those British monks. I knew him finally as a hollow, soulless creature with nothing truly Christian inside him. So I began to despise him.

Soon news arrived concerning the outcome of the synod. The Roman advocate, a priest named Wilfrid, had slyly derided the Irish in debate, asking with mock amazement how they and the British – inhabitants of a few remote and backward islands – could be so presumptuous as to oppose and contradict the opinions of all Christendom, and the very Church of St. Peter? As I had predicted, the Romans were triumphant and the Irish were forced to retreat, their customs rejected, their Church fatally weakened. And it seemed to me that while our Church was a glorious thing, the men who served it in these times often fell far short of glory.

Of course this victory was met with jubilation inside the monastery. I knew I lived under the constant surveillance of Adelard and his informers, so I went with care, giving no outward sign of my feelings in anything. This is the form my rebellion took. Self-concealment became my natural condition and suppressed rage my only companion as I withdrew into myself and grew suspicious of all those about me. I performed my duties adequately, to avoid accusations of obvious fault, but I did nothing more and shunned all company, not even communicating to others unless first addressed, and giving no more of myself in anything than I must. I distanced myself from the rest of the community until I came to see how hopelessly I had backed myself into a corner.

At that time a plague came to ravage the land, and for more than a year we were trapped inside the monastery, forbidden to venture outside for fear of contagion. And, thus isolated and restricted, the pressures in me grew, as the torments of doubt began to fester in my mind. I became ever more conflicted within, as I was haunted by horrible fears that I might be deeply in error and drenched in mortal sin. Could it be that the Devil had sown in me these seeds of resentment so that in my heart I defied the Church with that same anger and presumption with which Satan had opposed Heaven? Desperately I would pace my tiny cell in the night-time, a battle seeming to rage in my head, filling me with uncertainty and terror for the condition of my soul. Or I would awake from troubled dreams, my mind filled with the incoherent echoes of angry voices; or crying out in alarm as I imagined in the darkness that the walls of my cell were closing in upon me. In despair I did penance and mortified my flesh. I prayed constantly and feverishly for guidance. And I asked myself if all my torments were really only the conceits born of my stubborn pride?

It might have served me then to have accepted this; to have submitted and confessed my fault and sought absolution to end my pain. But finally I could not. For there remained inside me a lonely unbending voice that cried out: must my principles be pride? Might not my anger be righteous?

I was not ready for atonement.

So I remained alone, confiding my feelings to no one. As the state of my mind worsened, I knew that my life at the monastery had become insupportable and entirely detrimental to me, for I found no answers there. The place which had once been my home was now one of intolerable oppression and confinement to me. And I longed to be free of it: to find somewhere distant to still my mind. I was lost, terribly lost, and I knew I must find solitude to seek my reconciliation with God. So it was that I determined to lead a hermit's life – like the desert anchorites of old – in which I was certain I could feel no more alone than I did in that place.

At first my petition to the abbot was ignored. But I was persistent. For the place of my retreat I proposed the Fens – the most dark and inhospitable of regions – so that my intent might not be dismissed in any way as merely vain or frivolous. And at last Adelard relented.

So finally I came to stand once more before Abbot Adelard, on the eve of my departure, as he sat and regarded me coldly. His accusation that I was forsaking my duty to the Church stung me deeply and instilled in me a strong sense of guilt; but I saw how the monastery itself had come to seem like a metaphor for my very being. How could I hope to stand against the chaos of the world outside until I learned to contend with the turmoil within?

'And so, Brother,' he said, 'it is time for you to leave us. But first you will hear my judgement of you, for I think you stand in need of it. When you first came to us here, you became for a time a most promising member of this community. But your downfall has been your obduracy, which has become apparent in your excessive zeal. Ah, yes. It is true that a monk can be too zealous in his faith, I assure you. And it always displeases me to see this, for such a man is seldom reliable or sound. Remember that we must always be careful to bridle our faith with clear thought. This is what your Irish never understood, and that is why they lost. Common people may be impressed by displays of religious excess, but to thinking men such things are only the foolish posturing of children. I have often thought the title "saint" to be a distinction we bestow too freely upon attention seekers and lunatics. Yet I suppose these things please the simple folk and make them easier to manage. But you are not a simple man, Brother. So I caution you, do not fall so much in love with your own fervour that you mistake it for the true love of God. I have seen too many young monks divert their gross fleshly urges into what they delude themselves is religious passion.'

'I am hardly seeking to satisfy fleshly urges alone in the middle of a swamp,' I reminded him.

'Perhaps not,' he frowned. 'But I tell you plainly that while more impressionable men might see something to admire in your actions, I see only a man who would live without order, discipline or restraint.'

Inwardly I scowled at him. I could barely believe his words – that I was being rebuked inside a monastery for being overly religious.

'Now you may leave me,' he concluded. 'I wish you contentment, and bless your venture, Brother. Not because I approve of it, but because I would see you gone from here.'

Chapter Four

There were two servants – good carpenters and thatchers –
who went with me from the monastery, journeying up towards
the sea: to the great bay north of the Fens where lies the mouth
of the river called the Weolud which flows down through the
marshlands. We took with us a horse-drawn cart containing
our many items: building materials and implements, and my
own essential things, including sacks of grain and quern-
stones to make and burn my loaves of bread in the cinders of
the fire grate.

We travelled all that day over the flat bare plains of East
Anglia, the lands of the North-folk, dotted in every direction
with distant settlements, until at last we came within sight of
the faraway coastline as the day grew late and the light began
to fade. Then we turned from our course to enter the grounds
of a great estate where we might seek shelter for the night.
Soon we came upon a small group of dwellings, where several
of the cottagers greeted us, then took us onward to the hall of
their thegn, a grand manor house where a steward soon came
out to meet us.

'Lord Osric is away,' he informed us, 'summoned by the

king to Rendil's ham. But it is his instruction that men of the Church are always made welcome. I will have lodgings prepared.'

In the absence of the lord and his chief retainers the great hall seemed quiet and almost deserted as we were taken to a chamber annexed to the main building; and as we rested and warmed ourselves by the fire a servant brought us some bread and cheese for our supper. When we had eaten we began to settle our weary limbs for the night, but then there came a knock at the door, and the servant entered again and said to me:

'Lady Hild, the mother of Lord Osric, has asked if you will present yourself to her. She is very ill, near to death, and is confined to her chamber. Normally she will see no one. But she has asked to speak with you.'

I nodded my assent and followed him along a shadowy network of occasionally torchlit passages until we came to a closed door beyond which I could hear the soft chanting of women's voices as they sang what I took to be curative charms. Their tone was muted, so I could not tell if their words were Christian prayers or pagan spells, or even a combination of both. The kingdom of the East Angles had been converted to the Faith years ago, but sometimes the old customs survived barely disguised among the new.

My guide tapped on the door, and as a serving woman answered, I saw that the room inside was faintly lit, the air thick and pungent with smoking incense. I was led in, and as I entered the women who sat in attendance stopped singing, then rose and withdrew at once, leaving me alone with the lady herself, who sat wrapped in a dressing-gown of silver wolfskin. I gazed hard to see her, since her face was half hidden as she reclined in the shadows, yet it seemed to shine there with an almost translucent whiteness. Then she leaned forward into the light of a candle which stood on a small table by her side, dismissing the servant at the door with a nod as the glow further accentuated her extreme pallor; and I saw grey hair pulled back sharply from a face that was almost skeletal, the shrunken skin drawn tightly across the bones.

'I am Brother Athwold, lady,' I said, 'and I thank you for the hospitality we have received. How may I serve you?'

'How pleasant to welcome a guest,' she said in a voice that was faint and slightly slurred. It seemed that her eyes swam as she peered at me, and I realised she must be drugged and drowsy from a potion taken to ease her pain. She gave a smile, although in truth it was the grimace of a death mask, and even through the burning incense a cloying smell of sickness hung in the air. 'Your coming is fortuitous,' she announced. 'Soon I will die, and I wish to make a confession.'

'I am not a priest,' I told her. 'I cannot give you absolution.'

'No!' she agreed. 'But I hope you will listen to me and give me your counsel. I have long tried to be a good Christian, Brother. But as my time draws near I find suddenly there are doubts which trouble me. I wish to discuss them with you.'

'What is the nature of these doubts?' I said.

She gave a long sigh, and her breath rattled in her throat as she sank back into her chair.

'To explain this, I must speak of a time long ago, when I was young and first married, and the Faith of Christ was new to this land. Our first Christian king, Eorpwald, was murdered by a pagan usurper, and there was war in the kingdom between rival factions. But at last Sigbert came to be our king, returning from his long exile among the Franks and firmly imbued with their Christian beliefs. He was determined to convert the whole of East Anglia. Soon after his return a Frankish bishop arrived here on a progress through the land. His name was Felix.'

'Yes,' I said. 'Bishop of Dommoc, now gone to glory.'

'He came one day,' she nodded, 'with a retinue of priests and acolytes, and a formidable escort of armed men, to speak with the authority of the king. His preaching was filled with fire and also warning, and he left us in no doubt that compliance was demanded of us, as of all the noble families. There was much local opposition to this royal decree, and its harsh tone was resented, for until then we had been free to worship as we chose. Men asked how we might dare to abandon the beliefs of our ancestors which governed the cycle of the seasons and our traditional way of life. They looked to my husband's father, Lord Aldfrith, to give them leadership. But the memory of war was fresh in his mind, and he feared that if the kingdom should turn once more upon itself it would make us vulnerable to enemies beyond our borders. So, under the fierce eye of Bishop Felix, he conceded that we must accept the new Faith.

'His only son, my husband Oslac, was deeply affected by this. He was a fine young man of eighteen, good-natured, tall and handsome, his father's pride, and very devoted to the old gods. We had been married little more than a year, and had already been blessed by the birth of our son Osric, while a deep love had grown between us. But now he grew fretful, and remote even from me.

'Then one night I was disturbed in my sleep by Oslac rising from the bed and pulling on his clothes in the darkness. Barely awake, I asked what he was doing.

' "I must go," he answered in a strange sleepy tone. "There is a knocking at the door."

' "I heard nothing," I said. "Come back to bed."

' "I must go!" he said again.

' "Go where?" I asked him.

45

' "Outside!" he replied simply.

'It all felt like a dream to me, and I fell asleep again and knew no more until I woke at dawn to find him missing from our bed. I went to ask the servants where he was, but no one had seen him, and he was nowhere to be found. Now we grew alarmed, and his father began to organise a search-party for him.

'These men returned later, bringing Oslac with them. He was deathly pale, his clothes were soaked through, and he was frozen to the bone, for the night had been very cold. Lord Aldfrith questioned him, but Oslac barely replied or even acknowledged him, and seemed to be confused and lost in a kind of dreamlike state. The servants told us that he had been discovered in a far-off part of the estate, on the family burial ground, his body motionless and covered with white morning frost as he knelt on the hard ground beside one of the mounds, just staring blankly at it. By tradition the names of the ancestors buried in most of the graves were known, but the mound in question was very old, and the identity of its occupant long lost to memory. But one aged servant spoke of the belief that this mound contained the bones or relics of an ancient founder of the clan, steeped in old magic, brought long ago from across the sea and buried here by the first settlers.

'Oslac was put to bed, where he sank into a deep sleep, and for hours I sat with him, holding his hand and talking to him in the hope of reviving him. Until at last he awoke and looked up at me, then spoke in a voice that was faint and distant.

' "He came in the night... and I had to go with him. Out into the darkness."

' "Who came?" I said, relieved to see him animated again, but disturbed by his odd manner and words. "You must have been dreaming." Yet I was concerned, for I knew there were powers in the night which spoke to us in our dreams.

' "*No!* " he said. "It was not a dream. I went to his dwelling place and he stood there before me, finely clothed, his face fair and shining, radiant in the dark. He did not seem to speak, but his words came into my thoughts and said that for long ages he had served as our guardian and protector. In return we had given him our prayers and offerings, and sacrificed a fine ram to him every year in the Blood-month. But then his voice grew angry. *Why* – it demanded – would we now repay his faithfulness by forsaking him and sending him into exile?"

'Oslac had become feverish and as he raved these things sweat was streaming from him. Soon he fell back into an exhausted sleep. Desperate with worry, I went to Lord Aldfrith, but I found him in the company of Bishop Felix, who had somehow learned of Oslac's disappearance in the night. The bishop stood before me, looking down at me with sharp, hard eyes, then demanded:

' "What have you to report? Out with it, girl, and spare no detail if you value your husband's life and soul. And remember that I am here to represent the king. You will speak to me as you would address him."

'Thoroughly nervous, I stuttered out Oslac's words. When he had heard them, the bishop departed at once and went with a gathering of priests to the burial ground; and for the rest of the day they performed rituals and sang prayers and threw holy water over the ancient mound.

'That evening I climbed into bed beside Oslac and wrapped my arms about his shivering body to give him warmth, whispering to him of the bishop's efforts to drive away the spirit which tormented him – probably for my own comfort more than his, since he did not appear to be awake. Yet deep in the night I felt him stir, and once again he tried to rise from the bed, saying he must go to the one who called him. But I clung to him tightly to restrain him. Then he gasped out:

' "*He is here!* He has come to us." I felt my flesh quake, for it truly seemed to me that the air in our room at once grew deathly cold, and felt charged with a sense of unseen power. "But he is *changed!* He no longer shines, but is covered all over with a black cloak. His face is grown dark and angry, made raw and ugly with blisters. He says we have sent strangers to defile his sacred ground... and torture him with screaming spells and scalding water. He is no longer our friend and protector. He has become something vengeful... a *draug*... a demon from the death mound!"

'As I held him to me I felt his skin burning, and I knew his fever was reaching its height. I hurried from the bed and went to raise up the house. Lord Aldfrith said we must send for a priest to cast out the sickness, but all our old priests were gone, driven away by the Christians, so in desperation he sent word to Bishop Felix to come, although his magic was still foreign and strange to us.

'At daybreak the bishop arrived, clad in ceremonial robes and prepared for battle, accompanied by many priests and monks armed with crosses and censers and holy water. When I related Oslac's words to him, his eyes gleamed as he pronounced:

' "He is in dire peril. The Devil speaks through him. We must expel the forces of Satan to win his soul for Christ."

'I was trembling as I stood with Lord Aldfrith at the doorway to watch as the bishop and his clergy circled the bed and chanted in Latin, their voices growing louder and their gestures more dramatic, while Oslac lay seemingly unconscious, but restless and groaning in their midst, his features twisted and distraught. Until at last the bishop leaned over him, bringing his face close to Oslac's as he screamed out:

' "I compel you, devil, to depart in the name of Christ!" And the priests and monks began to intone these words, their voices rising like one.

'In a moment Oslac's eyes opened wide, looking huge in his pale, gaunt face as he stared with confusion and terror at the robed and hooded figures that stood gathered around him in the smoke-clogged chamber. His mouth fell open and his breath wheezed as the whole room fell quiet, and every eye was upon him, for at once there was something in his look that seemed to shine with a terrible lucidity. Then he croaked out in a voice so hoarse and strangled it was barely recognisable to me.

' "*You... are the devils!* Who come like thieves in the night to steal away the souls of my people... to defame and defile our sacred customs... and turn our nation's ancient faith and pride into something which is dark... and guilty... and *shameful*..."

'As he heard this the bishop's face grew enraged, and his voice rose like hate-filled thunder to denounce the blasphemy, while the priests and monks rushed forward like a screaming mob to close all about Oslac, shouting holy curses to drown out his voice and silence him. For what seemed a long time this went on. Until there rose above the din a long and dreadful cry. Then there was silence – a silence more awful to me than all the uproar which had gone before it.

' "The demon has fled, and in Christ we are triumphant!" I heard the bishop say at last. He turned towards us, yet his face was not exultant but desolate. "But I fear the ordeal has been too great for Lord Oslac. His malady has taken him. It is God's will, and the price of our victory." Then he moved aside to reveal Oslac, who lay sprawled and motionless, his eyes gaping lifeless in their sockets, his face rigid in a look of dying anguish.

'Behind me I heard the household start to wail and lament. I suppose I did too, although I do not remember it. But in my distress I did not believe it was the bishop who had won. I knew it was rather we who had lost, and broken faith with something deep and old in ourselves – the beliefs and traditions of our people which had served us since time beyond recall. The voice of our past had called to us, but for lack of courage we did not heed it, and so brought its wrath and vengeance upon us. It seemed to me then that in Oslac we mourned the lost spirit of our race. We had dispossessed them both together.'

Lady Hild fell silent, and her head nodded as she struggled to resist the soporific effect of her potion, clinging to consciousness as her eyes stared with a fierce intensity into the empty gloom behind me. At last she went on.

'For a long while in my heart I would not accept the new Faith, for to do so felt like a betrayal of Oslac's memory. But as time dulled my grief the world about me became wholly Christian, and gradually I lost the will and the rage inside to resist. So I tried to become a good Christian. But now, at the end, I doubt the wisdom of what I have done. I fear we have denied all that was once powerful and true in ourselves. And so it waits for us, beyond the veil of death, demanding *restitution.*'

Now I understood how she longed in death to be reconciled with the husband she believed she had failed. But he had died an unrepentant pagan and was therefore damned – on this the word of the Church was unyielding. I feared that guilt and remorse now brought her close to a lapse of faith. This was surely the reason she had sent for me.

'I assure you, lady,' I said, 'that the heathen deities and ancestral spirits we once revered were never real. They are illusions of the mind, false images sent by Satan to lure us far from the truth…'

'So you churchmen always say,' she answered with sudden vehemence. 'But you have lied to us. You cannot persuade me, Brother. I know the spirits are real. I see proof of it before me *now!*' She gazed out into the shadows beyond me, and I felt an icy thrill rush through my veins as I resisted a fearful urge to look over my shoulder. 'He comes to me,' she said fervently, 'each night, clothed in black, his face dark with anger and rebuke. It is he… *Oslac*… made bitter by my betrayal. *He has become the wrathful spirit!*'

'No!' I cried in desperation, reaching out to grip her hand. 'It is not Oslac. It is something demonic… a deception of the Devil! You must renounce it – *for the sake of your soul!*' Her sunken eyes stared past me into the dimness, but whatever she saw there now felt hideously real to me.

'I have heard such words before,' she whispered, 'from men like you. But you are the real deceivers.' Her voice rose suddenly. 'Husband… forgive me! I renounce my Christian faith… I set your spirit free!'

I looked on appalled as I clung to her hand, but I was losing her as she sank exhausted into a sleep from which she might never wake, her mouth creased into what was like the faint suggestion of a mocking smile. Was it for this she had summoned me – to stand as a witness to her terrible recanting? The sense of something imminent and utterly malefic filled the air and was now unbearable as blind panic gripped me and I turned and fled from the chamber in terror. And it seemed I heard the Devil laugh at me as I blundered lost and disorientated into the labyrinth of dark corridors outside.

I stood shaking as my fit of fear – whether real or imagined – subsided into deep feelings of mortification and defeat. At last I called out for the serving women, who came to return to their mistress and continued singing their dirge – which strangely I now recognised as a Christian psalm.

Chapter Five

The next morning I asked to be admitted once more into Lady Hild's presence, hoping in the light of day to find her in a more sound state of mind and to persuade her back from her dreadful apostasy. But I was told that now she lay insensible and close to death, and that a priest had been summoned on her behalf to perform the last rites. As I departed with my companions my mind was heavy with grief and shame at the memory of my abject conduct the night before and of how wretchedly I had failed both the lady and myself.

We reached the coast that morning, located a boat and loaded it with our items, and stabled our horse. We then set sail when the high waters came, and the boatmen rowed us inland to a place where the river diverged, navigating us along a winding tributary which meandered deep into the brooding marshes. Along the banks were the dirty huts and smallholdings of the sedge-men and reed gatherers, where we bartered to procure our materials for thatching.

At last we approached the dense woodlands which were the territory of the Crowland, and the boatmen leapt down into the water to steer the vessel onto the bank. From here we must drag our heavy cart across the marshes into the nearby woods. It was a gruelling task, and evening was upon us when finally we set up our camp among the trees close to my island. We ate our provisions in weary silence, then slept soundly in the open air, wrapped in our blankets as we lay around the fire.

The next day the two workmen – their names were Aelfwin and Ecfrith – cut down several tall trees and constructed from these a crude but functional log-bridge across the stream to carry our tools over onto the island, digging into the ground on either side and laying bases to make the structure secure.

Our work progressed quickly, and within days a simple dwelling took shape against one side of the solid burial mound. The two men at first seemed averse to using this old monument for their building foundation. I had expected this, for common men, even Christians, still carry in them the remnants of pagan superstition with regard to these mouldering barrows. But they soon became so absorbed in their work, and in overcoming the various difficulties which arose, that they seemed to forget about this.

My new habitation consisted of one main room, with the uneven protrusion of the mound as its far wall. Adjoined to this was the small room: my chapel, where I planned to spend most of my days, a plain cubicle with only a simple wooden cross fixed to its wall. For my furniture I had just a stool, and a palliasse and blanket in one corner as well as a spare robe, a wooden plate and cup, an iron pot to boil water and a knife, along with pumice stones to maintain my tonsure. These were my worldly goods.

We dug a hole into the mound and rearranged several of the heavy stones which lay upon it to construct a rough fireplace and a flue. We excavated nearby to create a covered pit, a cellar in which to store my supplies of grain.

One evening at sundown, when the dwelling was almost complete, I was sitting inside it when there came a sudden loud cry, a scrambling noise from above, then the sound of something outside striking the ground hard. I ran out to find it was Aelfwin, lying winded and dazed on the grass. He had been attending to some fault with the thatching when he slipped and fell. He was not hurt, but he was clearly frightened and distressed. As I helped him to his feet, he told me that from his vantage point on the roof he had looked across to the bank beyond the far side of the island and had seen there in the fading daylight, amidst the trees and the rising mist, a face that stared back at him, whose eyes, he said, had seemed to pierce his soul. He was white and trembling as he spoke.

I did not doubt that the isolation of this place and its gloominess, along with any irrational fears he might still harbour about disturbing the tumulus and angering the dead, were combining to work on his mind. So I attempted to reason with him.

'How can you be so certain of what you saw, in the darkness of the woods and in the mist?' I said. 'And I suppose even here we are not completely alone. There must be some others living on the fen, and I am sure our activities must have aroused their curiosity.'

'No, Brother, no!' He spoke as if I failed to understand. 'I tell you this was not like a man's face. It was something old. Something evil. *And it is watching us!*'

I could talk no sense into him. And I do not think he slept at all that night, for when I woke for my night-time prayers, I found him sitting upright and shivering in the dark.

The next morning the men started their labours even before I awoke, and they finished their outstanding tasks with great haste. Before noon they informed me their work was completed, gathered up their tools and wishing me God's blessing departed, heading back towards the river.

So now at last I was truly alone.

My first consideration, I supposed, should be my bodily sustenance. So I decided to make bread. To grind grain, make dough and bake bread is a laborious task, and not one I wished to repeat often, since it would distract me from my other concerns. So that day I made many loaves, but took only one to eat before sundown – I determined to allow myself no more than one loaf each day – storing the rest away. It would not bother me to eat stale bread.

But now my time of darkness truly began. In the weeks that followed I passed my hours in relentless contemplation and prayer, seeking to understand what it was that God asked of me. I knelt day after day in the confinement of my tiny chapel as the grim reality of a life of absolute solitude became clear to me. For now there were no others about me to be blamed for what I saw in myself, as I sank ever deeper into the agonies of inward terror and self-doubt. I was gone from the monastery, but its turmoil yet remained in me. I sought in my mind to balance the sins of anger and pride against the virtues of honesty and justice, and I asked myself what my true nature was. Was I at heart a man of goodness and inner strength, or just a weak, base creature of rage and resentment? But increasingly I could see only a blur, and I did not know. *I did not know.* Every certainty I had ever held was unravelling within me, and entirely alone I was losing all sense of myself. I only knew that if I could not tell the difference between virtue and sin, then I was truly damned.

Often I would fall to the ground in the midst of my devotions, beating my head there again and again, attempting to still the raging chaos within. But it seemed that God had abandoned me, and my demons were winning the battle, as I came to realise I was becoming a thing almost insane.

Once I reflected long upon those last words Abbot Adelard had spoken to me: that some monks concealed fleshly cravings behind their cries of love for God and deceived even themselves. Then I remembered my own confused feelings when Wecca had pulled me into his embrace. Filled with horror, I stripped off my robe and went to tear off a sapling branch, scourging my wicked flesh into the night.

I guessed it to be about the time of midsummer, when there came one of those occasional days when the mists cleared, the gloom lifted, and the sun shone. Shortly before sundown I emerged from my chapel after a day of torment, feeling so weary that I had become dull in my senses and almost calm. I took my daily repast of one dry loaf and a cup of water to sit and consume them by the bank of the stream. But as I settled there I became aware of the sound of a vigorous splashing somewhere in the water nearby. This was the first sign of any life I had encountered since coming here.

Curious, I began to walk along the bank, looking out into the stream. But I saw nothing until suddenly a human head burst up out of the water. I stared in startled astonishment, for I saw then the face of a dark-haired and pretty young woman, perhaps seventeen, who smiled over at me unexpectedly. Without thinking I smiled back – the first time I had smiled at anyone for as long as I could remember. Her eyes sparkled at mine for several moments, then she plunged back under the water, and I glimpsed her bare white skin as she dived. After a few moments she resurfaced, now closer to me. I reached forward, holding out my loaf of bread to her, for this seemed a friendly gesture, and the bread was good and fresh that day. She stared for a few moments at my offering, then swam towards the bank, and for an instant she pulled herself up out of the stream to take the bread from me. I felt a sudden sense of shock, then a fluttering sensation in my stomach and a quickening of my heart as she rose naked before me, her breasts small and firm, her body lithe and glistening with the droplets of water running down it. Then she slid back under the surface.

I stood feeling restless and awkward as she crouched in the stream and grinned at me between mouthfuls of the bread. When she had finished, she spoke a few words to me in a light, almost laughing voice, in a language I did not understand, yet which sounded somehow familiar. I felt then that I must try to communicate with her, to tell her and make her see that it was not proper for her to show herself to me in this way. But in that moment it did not seem to me so very wrong, but only a natural lack of inhibition and self-consciousness that suggested no awareness in her that it could be wrong. Perhaps I was simply too exhausted to respond as I felt I should. And anyway I could think of no innocent way for me to try to make her aware of her own natural state. But my casual attitude surprised me, for I had been taught to regard young women – even fully clothed ones – as the Devil's temptresses. Yet this girl appeared simply wild and innocent, and her presence charmed me. There definitely seemed to be nothing of the Devil about her.

She giggled slightly, then gestured to herself and said 'Ailisa'. This was clearly her name, so I tapped my own chest and answered 'Athwold'; and she repeated it back to me. We remained there for a time, simply seeming to enjoy each other's presence. Then, too soon, she waved her hand at me, swam back out into the stream, and was gone.

I sat for a short while and felt lighter in spirit than I

believed I had been since I was a child. And I realised now that Ailisa's speech had seemed recognisable to me because it had resembled a dialect of the Celtic tongue that I had occasionally heard spoken in my younger days. But of course this confirmed my idea that native Britons still inhabited these Fenlands in small groups, descendants of hidden tribes or perhaps runaway slaves. I was happy to see that Ailisa did not seem to fear me or bear me any animosity, since normally the Britons show much hatred towards the Angles and Saxons. I was also relieved to have seen at first hand that these people were certainly in no way monstrous or deformed, as Wecca's fearful ramblings had seemed to suggest.

But soon the darkness returned to blot out this brief ray of light. Each day I continued with my struggle, as my torments grew worse, and slowly I felt the demons of my doubts gnaw ever deeper into my soul, while God continued to turn the light of His countenance from me. Yet now, late each afternoon, I would emerge from my chapel and go with my daily loaf to sit beside the stream, hoping she would return. Until one day soon, as I rested on my spot by the water's edge, I heard her voice somewhere distant, calling out my name. I saw her on the opposite bank, dressed now in a garment of animal hide, and she carried over her shoulder a stick, from which there hung by its mouth a good-sized fish. I smiled as I walked along level with her, the stream between us, until she came to my bridge, crossing over it and coming to stand before me, while she held out the fish as an offering.

She sought to make me a gift in return for the bread I had given her. I made an extravagant gesture of thanks, then gave her another poor offering of my bread; and we sat together for a while, attempting to communicate as we exchanged shy glances. I was much touched by her gift and had not the heart to refuse it, although I was sworn to eat only plain bread here, and I buried the fish untouched later that night.

After this she began to visit me often, always around the same time, and together we devised a game in which we would exchange our different words for all the things we pointed to around us; and soon a kind of rudimentary language, a jumble of words from both our tongues, started to develop between us. I began to like Ailisa more than I could say – not just for her pale skin, dark eyes and her ready laugh, but also for her quickness to learn, as in our games she soon proved sharper than me. I knew well that my masters in the Church would have denounced my friendship with her and doubtless suspected my motives for it. But I truly could see nothing wrong in it, innocent as I knew it to be. I was aware by now that this distraction and respite from the gloom of my solitary existence could only be beneficial for me. And also for Ailisa, living somewhere nearby with her small family of exiles, as I suspected her own life could be barely less lonely than mine. In fact I knew now that Ailisa had become the single spark of light in all my darkness, and I did not care even to imagine existing there without her.

But the day quickly came when I grew troubled by our companionship. It was as we played and laughed together at our word game that our eyes met, and there was a moment of sudden intensity between us, as she moved closer to me, and I was stricken by an overpowering urge to reach out and take her in my arms. In that instant I could feel that love was growing between us. But I held back with a sense of shock as I knew this could not and must not be. I was a monk vowed to celibacy, who stood upon the brink of damnation, locked in a daily struggle to redeem my soul. Yet how could I explain these things to Ailisa? How would I ever make her understand them? I saw then that the admonishments of the Church were wise. How might I tell her I could never be her mate, nor offer her that love which is natural between woman and man?

In the nights that followed I began to suffer the onslaught of oppressive dreams, which came upon me in suffocating waves of sensual horror: the secret creeping urges of restless and illicit desires, the imagined intimacy of soft and sultry flesh, of something faceless in the dark, and hands which stroked and clung to me, and gave thrilling caresses which overcame all my strength and resistance, to draw me helplessly into their deeper embrace. And I would awake with such a burning in my flesh tormenting me that it was as if I were already lost within the fires of Hell. Once I dreamed a vision of Ailisa, as I had first seen her, rising up naked and gleaming from out of the water; but here it seemed she was subtly transformed into something unlike herself – something lustful, and brazen in her nakedness, her mouth soft and wet as she ran her tongue lazily over her full lips, her dark eyes provocative and coldly wanton as she stared at me. And in the daytime, when next she came to me, and I looked into her face – sweet, smiling and wholly ingenuous – I knew that her image in my dream was only a wild phantasm from the wicked depths of my own imagination, a corrupt and unwholesome inversion of all that was real and true. Then I began to fear that perhaps after all Ailisa was unwittingly one of the Devil's subtlest snares.

I realised now that I must find strength and courage to end our friendship. It would be hard to do. Indeed it would be terrible. But there was no other way, for it would be deleterious to me and unfair to Ailisa to let this matter continue. I wondered if perhaps this was a trial God had set for me as a test of my faith.

My conduct in all this only gave me further cause to suffer and reproach myself. I had thoughtlessly allowed this situation to occur, and now in seeking to correct it I feared I must hurt Ailisa terribly. It was all as a consequence of my own selfishness. But finally I became reconciled to what must be, and in the late summer I determined that when Ailisa visited me the next day, I must tell her she should come no more.

It was fittingly a chilly dismal day, and the rain had been falling relentlessly when I stood beside my bridge – soaked and dejected – to await her arrival.

But that day she did not come.

Unsettled and frustrated, but secretly relieved, I wandered back to my shelter; and I thought at last to eat my ration of bread. I found that only a few loaves remained in my store and told myself absently that I must make some more. But when I took out a loaf I saw that it had started to spoil from the heavy peculiar dampness which often rises to pollute the atmosphere in the Fens. On the crust there had formed the beginnings of a black mould. I carelessly took my knife and scraped away the worst of this, then softened the bread in my cup of water before eating it. Then I lay on my bed to reflect miserably on my expected meeting with Ailisa the following day and the extinction of my life's only happiness.

But instead I fell asleep almost at once. Yet I awoke again soon after in the realisation that something was wrong – that something was happening to me. My head felt light, and I could not think clearly, as the room appeared to spin about me. I wondered vaguely if I might have contracted a marsh fever. But I was suddenly transfixed when I looked across at the dim glow of the dying fire in my hearth. For it seemed to my eyes that the tiny flame assumed a life of its own. Golden and red streaks appeared to rise up from it, waves of vibrant colour that shimmered astonishingly in the dark. Then the surrounding blackness itself seemed to join in these wild motions, swirling and weaving into the light to create a myriad of drifting, shifting patterns. I cannot say how long I lay there, entranced by this amazing vision, which seemed to me to be purely angelic, before I drifted back into sleep.

Chapter Six

When I awoke the next day I seemed fully restored to my normal state. There were certainly no signs of any fever or sickness in me. Yet I regarded my nocturnal vision – or was it a half-sleeping and half-waking dream? – as an encouraging sign, for its beauty had seemed to be an omen of the light. But then my thoughts turned to Ailisa, and the vision was quickly forgotten. The rain had stopped and the day looked mild, and I knew that later she would come. I found I could not concentrate my mind on anything that day, for I dreaded her coming and what must be our final meeting. And I anticipated with bleak despair the prospect of my future life, spent here alone without ever seeing her again. I could barely imagine what was to become of me.

At the usual time she arrived, waving her hand to me and smiling in greeting. But as she crossed the bridge and approached me, my troubled state must have been apparent to her, for she began to regard me with concern.

'No bread?' she said with surprise, for it had been my usual custom since our first meeting to give her such an offering when she came, as my only available token of friendship and welcome. I shook my head dully, and her face grew sad. It seemed she thought I had no food, and must go hungry that day.

We sat together on the grass, and at once I was at a loss. I did not know how to begin to explain the matter to her. My message would have been a difficult one to convey even to someone who shared my own language and understanding of the world. But to speak it here, to this innocent girl who had spent her whole life in these wild Fens, and in the crude parlance we had barely started to construct together, seemed an impossible and devastating task. Seeing my distress, Ailisa reached out to place a comforting hand upon my arm, and gave a smile to encourage me, utterly disarming me and making all my sorrow and irresolution still worse.

Then, as I began to attempt to speak, I was interrupted by the sound of several harsh voices that rose from somewhere distant to break the silence over the fen. Ailisa's response was immediate, her body stiffening as she sprang to her feet, gazing out into the direction from where the shouts had come, seeming almost to search the air itself. She turned to me, clearly alarmed, and reached out to clutch at my hand. We had not yet devised a common word for danger, but it seemed now there was no need for one.

'Go! Go in house!' She spoke urgently as she pointed to my shelter. 'You stay. Stay inside. This night you go *ssh!*'

I stood staring at her, a little confused by her excited state, since the voices had seemed to me to come from somewhere far away. But I knew that bands of outlaws sheltered in parts of this great wilderness: violent and dangerous men who went out to raid the villages by night. Clearly Ailisa had learned to be cautious. With a final look at me, and another frantic gesture towards my refuge, she turned and ran back over the bridge, and I watched her go until she disappeared amongst the trees. Then I did as she had urged me and went indoors.

I heard no further sounds from out in the fen. So I sat in weary disconsolation, turning my awful predicament over and over in my thoughts. Until finally I noticed that the night-time shadows had fallen, and I remembered I had eaten nothing. I had no appetite, but almost without thought I took another loaf from out of my depleted stock – I had been too preoccupied to think of making any fresh ones. But I noticed at once that this loaf had become far more deeply infested with mould than the bread I had eaten the day before, to the extent that I could no longer scrape or cut it away. But this was the least thing to concern me, and I considered that it had not previously harmed me, so I simply ate it quickly, ignoring the bitter taste, then washed it down with a draught of water.

I sat for a short while, then looked out through the half-open door at the dim beams of moonlight that faintly penetrated the rising mist. And as I watched the shafts of glowing light they seemed suddenly to greatly increase and brighten with a strange and remarkable sharpness. I was feeling light-headed, then positively dizzy, with an incredible and heightened awareness of myself and of my surroundings as this new intense world of increased vision emerged from out of the greyness of the one I knew.

It was happening to me again. A realm of altered perceptions was opening before me, a wondrous place of elevated sight and realisation. It seemed then that the light I had long prayed for had come to me, and a wave of pure euphoria swept through me as I dared to hope that at last my long path of darkness and doubt had led me to this: to walk in the brightness of a heavenly place where I might be cleansed of the dross and mire of my earthly life. In that moment I felt certain God held out His hand to me.

I rose and stumbled to the door, going out into the night, entranced by all I saw about me: a shifting swirling landscape of interweaving moonlight and shining silver mist, becoming threaded into the night shadows to form fleeting transitory shapes ahead. I staggered after them, as if to catch them, unable to keep my steps in a straight line as I moved unsteadily through this rising forest of enchantments that would not stay still but appeared to alter and reshape itself constantly in ever-deepening shades and hues of vibrant colour.

Somewhere in my mind I remembered Ailisa and that there was something I must tell her, but I could not recall what it was. As the sight of my log-bridge swam before my eyes, I decided irrationally that I must go out into the fen to find her. Unsteadily I managed to totter across it and wandered away among the trees, which began to spin about me in a kind of mad and twirling jig. I was dimly aware that I had roamed beyond the woods, and I stumbled about on the edge of some marshes, and the noise from the tall reeds as I brushed through them seemed to scream out in my head. But now I came to realise that my delirium was becoming ever more violent and wild, and what had seemed at first to be subtle and intriguing was growing into something uncontrollable and frightening as the earth and the sky began to lurch and reel crazily about me. I was almost lost to all physical feeling, and I sensed I was about to crash helplessly to the ground when I saw through the rushes far away the glow of a great shining light. And by some force of will I kept moving towards it, convinced that the distant stirrings of fear and alarm in me must surely be a sign that I approached a manifestation of the divine – as the Lord had called to Moses from inside a burning bush.

As I went on and the light grew nearer, it became ever more

overwhelming to me, flaring outward in great fiery waves and colours, shooting sparks and flames that filled the earth and the sky, and whose heat I could feel burning upon my skin from far away. Until at last I came before it, seeing it clearly as I stood enraptured, my gaze fixed adoringly on its blazing beauty. Then my eyes grew wider still, as my nostrils were suddenly flooded with the overpowering smell of roasting flesh. There were noises now, rising up from the gloom beyond the firelight – a horrible chorus of harsh laughter and guttural cries, cracked and growling voices whose words I could not comprehend. At once I saw several shadowy forms, black and sinister figures creeping forward to surround me, and I felt a jolt of confusion, then of panic and terror. I flung myself away from them, stumbling backward, uttering a loud cry as my arms flailed and I tripped, falling to the ground at their feet. There came from them a further burst of vile, coarse laughter as they stared down at me, and I looked up into their faces in horrified disbelief.

These creatures were not human, but things that were wholly monstrous. Their faces – if faces I might call them – were hideously distorted, blazing bright red in the glow of the fire. The flesh and features were impossible for me to distinguish clearly, for they blurred before my tortured eyes, seeming to swell and contract constantly, as if boiling from underneath like thick porridge bubbling in a pot. When they mouthed their grating words at me, it was not like any speech I could recognise, but only more of that obscene and throaty grunting, while their lips were like shapeless gashes filled with crooked yellow tusks. One of them stepped forward now, reaching down to me as its hand seemed to float and circle in the air before me, until I felt certain I could see that its fingers were clawed. It grasped my robe by the neck and pulled me back onto my feet, and I was surrounded on all sides by dreadful leering masks of vileness, all bellowing what I took to be curses at me with breath that stank like stale beer and spittle that flew into my face.

Then I realised I had been hurled back to the ground, and one of the creatures was approaching me, calling to me in a tone filled with mockery. Its voice was shrill, and I took it to be female. I felt it thrust its clammy hand up into my robe to grab painfully at my lower parts; and then it was squatting over me, pulling up its garment and thrusting its filthy pudenda into my face as it wiggled its hips, the stink of the thing musky and rank as it shrieked out incomprehensible taunts at me. My head was spinning, and I felt I was falling, plunging into darkness as I tried desperately to crawl away. But I was seized by my legs and dragged back into the blinding light of the fire. Then I felt a hot stinging sensation on my shoulders, and I knew suddenly that another of the monsters was pissing on me.

In some distant corner of my mind I believed now I understood everything. I saw at once with fearful clarity that I was dead and that my life had slipped away silently back in my hut on the island, and that it was my soul which had wandered here, entranced by all its newly found powers of unearthly vision. In joy I had seen the possibility of Heaven but found only the reality of Hell. And this was surely why a human spirit possessed these heightened perceptions: that it might know forever with absolute intensity the pleasures of paradise or the torments of perdition. I gazed up at the foul demons who persecuted me, and I began to wail dismally as I told myself that God had passed His dreadful judgement on me, and what I suffered now was all I should know evermore throughout eternity itself.

It was then, in that final moment of my hopelessness, that

I saw another figure rise up, looming like a phantom out of the mist, a form more terrible and ominous than all the rest as it gathered shape to move, silent and unseen by those others who stood jeering at me. I froze as I gazed upon this unearthly shade, swathed all over with darkness and of a towering height. And in my dread I could only believe it to be Satan himself. Writhing tendrils of fear sprang up from the pit of my being and broke into dull bursts of stultifying shock which pulsed and pounded through my brain, while it felt as if a cold giant hand closed hard about me. I could distinguish nothing about the approaching figure, for it appeared to be a thing formed out of pure blackness, framed in the leaping light of the flames. A spirit of fire. And of terrifying *rage*.

In an instant it raised a black arm, which seemed abnormally long, then brought it down with tremendous force onto the skull of one of my tormentors; and I watched simply spellbound as an eruption of shining redness streaked into the night and looked to my eyes to hang in the air in sluggish glistening droplets. Then the demon was falling, and the powerful arm of the shadow slashed out into the throat of another. Their fellows were screaming and stumbling as howling chaos descended. But the dark one was relentless as it struck about it with deadly power, and the devils fell dead or wounded as they bellowed out their dreadful cries of terror. I saw the she-devil start to flee, but the shade struck her in her back, and she squealed piteously as she fell, then attempted to crawl away with hideous slithering motions before at last she grew still. For one moment, in the midst of this, I felt the gaze of the dark one upon me, and I sensed its pure, savage fury, before it moved on to dispatch another of the floundering wounded.

Suddenly sheer dread pulled me to my feet, and I was racing off into the darkness, fleeing that place of carnage and horror, knowing that my mind could not contain such terror but was surely tumbling into a pit of shrieking madness. As I went my senses grew more wildly distorted than ever, my surroundings rising and plunging about me as if I tried to run upon a boat in a great storm. Now it came to me that I did not know what or where I was, if I were alive or dead, man or spirit… earthbound or in Hell… I simply struggled to keep moving, fearing the pursuit of that dark and murderous thing in the firelight. I could not imagine what kind of horror it was, but somewhere in my tormented brain I asked myself how it was possible for anything to kill demons in Hell? I could no longer guess what it was I was experiencing.

At once I stumbled and fell face-down onto the soft damp earth, and there I scrabbled in a frantic effort to rise to my feet until my swirling senses overcame me and I sank back down again, lying motionless as pure terror finally made me powerless. For behind me I heard the soft, slow padding of feet, and there came to me the dreadful certainty that the horror was now standing over me. I shuddered and could not bring myself to look upward, to gaze upon it finally and see it more clearly. But from some place within myself I heard my own voice rise up, my breath groaning, the words straining inside the rigid muscles of my throat as involuntarily I croaked them out into the night air.

'In nomine patris et filii et spritus sancti.'

For what seemed an age I lay there, awaiting the awful fate I was certain must come.

But nothing happened. Until at last I fought to gather courage to turn my head and look behind me. I was quite alone. So I rose and staggered onward, fearing every moment what new horror might emerge at me from out of the mist. Then with incredible relief I saw through the gloom beyond me the bridge to my island. I ran to it and fell to the ground, gripping the frame of rough logs to convince myself that this was reality and no false illusion of hope sent to torment me. On hands and knees I scrambled across it, then stumbled up to my dwelling. Everything there was as it should be, and I felt a sudden surge of absolute joy at its plain familiarity. I was not in Hell. I was in the Fens. And I was alive.

I fell onto my bed and lay shivering in the dark. My vision was still blurred and my senses remained in a state of spinning turmoil as I considered the horrors I had experienced. It seemed mercifully that I remained as a part of the living world, but if the horrible creatures I had encountered were not demons in Hell, then what were they? Wild men? Monsters in the fen? That was not possible. The Church had taught me that such things existed only in the minds of the superstitious and foolish. Somewhere in my disordered senses I was becoming aware that something must have affected me, and I wondered again if I were the victim of some fever or brain sickness. Such afflictions were no doubt common in these marshes. Some part of me at once became certain this must be so – that what I had suffered was only a hallucinatory vision or delusion: a frenzied, walking nightmare. I told myself with relief that this was the only credible explanation. But then I considered the dark and hellish scenes my imagination had created and felt little comforted as I asked myself what these awful things might suggest about the true state of my mind?

Then suddenly I became aware that I was lying in a clammy patch of dampness. And with a feeling of disgust, but then of extreme horror, I realised that the back of my robe was soaked with a great stain of stinking urine.

Chapter Seven

My mind was numb as I struggled to pull off the soiled robe and cast it away into the far corner of the room, wishing I could discard as easily the things it suggested to me. Shock pulsed through me as I fumbled in the darkness to find my cloak and wrap it about me. Then I tumbled back onto the mattress and lay shivering in the shadows. What was it I had truly encountered out in the fen? What had been real, and what was illusory? No answer came, only the same question repeating itself to me with a relentless and horrible monotony.

I began to pray, silently and feverishly, wishing the night would end and that with the dawn of day normality would be restored and with it my power to think coherently, for at present all clear thought was denied to me. Now my whole being was consumed by a sickening terror of the soul, and I lay paralysed with the fearful sense that if I should make a movement or a single sound then something outside – *something grim and malevolent* – might hear it and come for me. And I knew that if such an unearthly presence did come, and I should look upon it and know it as a thing of reality, then my every belief, every certainty I held in the world, would tumble down and break into fragments at my feet, to leave me helpless in the face of darkness.

I lay a long while until at last my skin began to prickle and grow tight, and my heart started to thump painfully as my breath rose in great gasps I could no longer hold in. For again I could hear with uncanny sharpness the sound of soft padding footsteps, which broke the absolute silence outside, and approached, stealthily yet inexorably, and seemed to tread around – *or else to come from within* – the tumulus itself. I felt something break inside me then, as if the farthest limit of my fear had been finally breached, and now I did not know, *could* not know, what might exist beyond it. What stood outside.

For the monster was here. It was at my threshold.

The door crashed open and it loomed before me in the dim moonlight, its great black frame filling the doorway, its immenseness overshadowing me. Out in the fen it had seemed like a thing of fire, but here it was a thing of ice, as the faint beams of light rippled over its gigantic shape to make it glow with a cold and spectral aura of blue. But still I could make out nothing about it even as it moved before me, for it was a creature of absolute darkness, and its body glistened like polished jet. My mind was beyond all rational power as I looked upon it, and the dreadful presence suddenly lurched forward, hurling itself at me as I screamed out, its form appearing to grow blurred and swell absurdly into a shapelessness that swallowed the room and filled my vision – a devouring darkness that fell over me and would utterly consume me. Now I felt the supreme horror of its touch on my quivering flesh, its fingers hideously strong and hard like talons as they descended upon my breast, clawing agonisingly into skin and sinew. Its sheer power overwhelmed me, as did my very sensing of it, a thing black and old as night, a monstrosity born out of stinking slime and eternal chaos. But still, beyond the crippling terror in my mind, my body stirred instinctively into motion as I fought and struggled against it with a frantic strength, beyond any I knew was mine, for it seemed to me suddenly that I was fighting desperately for something more than merely my life. Yet slowly my strength was failing me, for the sheer force of the horror was irresistible, its weight upon me crushing; and in moments I knew it would squeeze the life from out of me. But as my senses began to slip away, there came the dreadful certainty that even in death I could never break free: that this thing of darkness would surely tear through my sinner's flesh to fix its terrible grip upon my eternal soul. And with this thought there seemed to boom out in my head a harsh and mocking voice that cried:

'You fool! Do you not see? What clings to you is not what would steal your soul. *It is your soul!*'

It was at that moment that I realised I was dreaming.

I woke with a start, to see daylight streaming into my dwelling. I felt weak and very cold, and I was sweating profusely, but there came a moment of indescribable relief as my waking mind roused itself, striving to break free from the fearful visions of sleep. Then I looked upward, and my heart squirmed as shock and terror struck me anew, as I saw through blurred eyes the awful figure of darkness from my dream transposed into living reality, its fierce gaze fixed upon me as it stood framed in the dull light at the open doorway, and the frightful realisation came: *it had pursued me into the waking world.*

I lay transfixed as my sight grew clearer, until I saw that what stood before me was indeed quite real, but was mercifully the figure of a man: a monk of commanding presence dressed in a mud-stained cloak over the dark habit of my own Benedictine order. He was perhaps about forty, of middle height and sturdy frame, his face rugged, his expression very severe. His eyes were a deep brown in colour, as were his hair and short ragged beard, though the latter was flecked with grey. Upon his breast was a bronze cross – usually a prerogative reserved for an abbot – wrought with a circle around its centre in the Celtic fashion, which hung from a chain about his neck. I tried to speak, but was for the moment too shaken and astonished to find any words. Then a voice came from behind me.

'You have eaten bad bread!' I turned abruptly to see a second figure inside the gloom of my dwelling. A young man, fair-haired and handsome in the way of the Angles. He wore a green tunic and to his back were strapped a travelling-bag and a spear. I saw then that he held the sack which had contained my bread loaves, and in his hand he raised the last loaf, now black with mould, and went on: 'It is the growth upon your bread which has affected you. You must take care in these Fenlands, for they are not like any place you have known before. The air here is sometimes a cause of strange effects.'

At once I understood him, and with his words my mind flooded back into vivid memories of my visions in the night. I knew it was the practice of pagan shamans and wonder-workers to use certain natural growths, plants and fungi, to create altered states of mind. They claimed this was a passage into the world of spirits. But the Church condemned the use of these substances, dismissing their effects as mere hallucination and temporary insanity. Once more I began to pray that all the things I had seemingly witnessed had been only illusions and febrile dreams. But as I lay wrapped just in my cloak and saw my soiled robe discarded on the floor, I felt deep within me a horrible doubt that this could be so, and I wondered again what parts of my terrifying remembrances might be real.

'Forgive our intrusion, Brother,' said the young man with a friendly smile. 'Our path has led us here, where we came upon you sleeping and feverish. We are on a mission of great urgency and importance, by command of Ecbehrt, lord of the Gyrwas people, and we are charged as we go to make sure of the safety of inhabitants of these lands.'

'And to question them.' Now the monk spoke, and his voice was deep and resonant, and carried a strange accent that sounded lilting and almost musical. 'To determine if they have knowledge of any recent *disturbances*.' He laid emphasis on this last word as he raised an inquiring eyebrow.

'Last night,' I gasped out, finding my voice at last. Even as I spoke the words it seemed to me clearly a thing beyond coincidence that these strangers should have arrived here at this time – that their presence was somehow related to my night-time experiences. 'I went out onto the fen... and I saw...' I shook my head, for I could not tell truly *what* I had seen '...I fear... I fear it was something *terrible!*' I concluded miserably.

At once the monk strode to my side, flint-faced as he stared down at me.

'*What did you see?* Tell me now.'

'Monsters!' I groaned. 'To my eyes they looked like... monsters. They attacked me. But then something else attacked them. Something worse... more horrible and monstrous still. But I had eaten the bread... the bad bread. I understand now that I saw nothing clearly or truly, that my wits were unbalanced and my sight distorted.'

The monk turned from me and spoke to the other man.

'You must trace his path out into the marshes. We must learn the truth of this.'

Together they departed from my dwelling, with no further words to me. Hurriedly I pulled on my spare robe, intent on going with them, for I too must know the truth of these things. But first, with a sudden sense of fear and foreboding at the prospect of venturing back out onto the fen, I felt a need to carry with me a thing for my comfort of mind and my protection. And I went to my chapel to take down from the wall my small cross, and held it to my breast as I hurried out after them.

Already they had crossed over the bridge, and in the dull morning light the younger man was searching the ground for signs of my tracks. Almost at once he was moving forward, darting to and fro among the trees, and as I approached them he called back to me without looking around.

'A twisted path, but see – your wanderings are easy to follow. You blundered like a lame boar. Much dangerous in these marshlands.'

'My name is Brother Athwold,' I said, looking at the monk as I came to walk at his side. 'Please tell me what is your mission. What are you doing here?'

He turned his head to look at me, his gaze at once hard and intense, but we had left the cover of the trees and were moving out into the marshes before he spoke.

'I might ask you the same question. What is it that would induce a young monk to abandon his home and his brothers in Christ to seek exile in such a place?'

'I came here to find God... and myself,' I answered cautiously, for I felt I detected in his voice a note of disapproval, and at once he firmly reminded me of Abbot Adelard.

'Then you look for God in a land that is godforsaken,' he muttered. 'For all that there are now Christian settlements upon the larger Fenland islands, most of the native fen-men still cling obstinately to the old ways. Do not doubt it is the Devil who rules here.'

'Then you are a missionary?' I said.

'I am Brother Cadroc,' he replied – probably a British name – 'and my companion is Aelfric, a ranger of these lands, appointed by Ealdorman Ecbehrt to be my guide here.'

Now we fell silent while I felt a vague sense of resentment at what I perceived to be Brother Cadroc's judgemental manner, disguising itself as Christian righteousness. It was a form of self-regard I had known in other churchmen, who deceived themselves into believing it a genuine concern for the welfare of others. But then I saw that my own attitude was unjust. The fact was that here in this place, Brother Cadroc represented the scrutiny and appraisal of the Church, from which I had lately been exempt, and to which I must now learn once more to submit myself. What I felt in truth was a growing sense of apprehension at the thought of what I might find in the marshes ahead, for while my attackers in the night had seemed wholly monstrous to my eyes, yet I hoped my eyes had been deceived, for the Church had told me such monsters did not exist, and all that was rational in my mind was intent on believing this. It felt almost as if my faith itself depended on it. But as there came to me the dreadful recollection of that huge and shadowy figure, spreading death all about it, a deep fear and uncertainty filled my heart, for it seemed to my every underlying sense that what I had seen, however deranged my perceptions, simply could not have been human.

'There!' Aelfric called out, pointing ahead. His pace quickened, and as I followed him a feeling of shock and numbness fell upon me as I saw among the reeds a corpse lying prostrate, half submerged in a pool of mud and blood. As we came to it, I observed that its head was twisted to one side, the face partly exposed, and a swelling of nausea and dread rose in me as I gazed upon it, and the worst of my fears was realised. For it was surely the face of nothing human, but a vile and disfigured thing of the utmost horror, its black misshapen features grotesquely swollen about a giant gaping maw filled with blood and shattered teeth.

'There are others!' Cadroc said, moving onward. A short distance beyond lay four more bodies, scattered about the burnt-out remains of a fire, over which hung the charred carcass of an animal, and I knew beyond doubt that this was the place I had chanced upon in the night. But as I began to study the carnage some part of me felt almost a sense of relief, for it soon became clear to me that these corpses, beneath all their horrible mutilations, were those of men – if one might call such savages men. My tormentors had been common outlaws – filthy and debased creatures, certainly, but undeniably *human*. Then I understood that the first corpse we had discovered had been likewise only a man, whose face had been simply ripped apart. And as I looked about me at these others, their lifeless expressions stricken with terror, their flesh slashed and mangled by great raking wounds; then glanced with a shudder at the body of the woman who had mocked me, lying face-down with the flesh on her back torn into shreds, it seemed to me almost as if the injuries inflicted here had not been done by any weapon of man, but appeared more like the crazed ravages of *giant claws*.

'We are still upon the trail,' Cadroc said to Aelfric at last, 'and our task grows ever more desperate.' I began to stumble away, feeling sick and unable to bear the distressing scene any longer. But Cadroc came after me saying: 'You must tell us what it was you saw. What do you recall? I must inform you that you are so far the only witness to the terror who has survived it.'

'I told you I remember only confusion!' I cried out, growing frantic with alarm to have seen the dreadful fate I had so narrowly escaped. 'It is you who must tell me what it is I have witnessed. *Tell me what has happened here!*'

'I have no time,' Cadroc said, turning away. 'My path calls me onward and I cannot delay.'

'Look!' Aelfric called out, standing nearby and pointing to the ground. I went with Cadroc to his side and felt a shudder ripple through me as I saw there in the watery sludge what looked to be the faint outline of a footprint, yet one that seemed to be of truly enormous size, surely bigger than that of any man I had ever seen. And yet, I sought to reassure myself, the print was too vague to be certain of this. But then I noticed that I held my cross in both hands, and had come to grip it so tightly that it hurt my fingers. Slowly I slipped it into the pouch inside my robe.

'We go on!' Cadroc declared firmly. With this, both men simply began to walk away from me. But I hurried after them, calling out:

'Brother! Wait! After what I have suffered you cannot leave me like this, without explanation.'

Cadroc gave me a glance filled with impatience, but then something in him seemed to change, and his look became milder as he turned to me and said:

'Forgive my discourtesy, Brother Athwold, but I fear my task consumes me to the detriment of all other considerations. Walk with us if you will, and I will tell you what I know. It may be my words will help to stir your memories.'

So we set off, Aelfric going in front to guide us along the winding pathways through the marshes. I had never ventured far from my hermitage before and feared that my journey back home through these wild swamps might be difficult. Yet I must know the things this man Cadroc had to impart. I must learn the truth of this awful matter to which by misfortune I had been a witness.

'You have seen,' Cadroc began, 'that a thing of great evil haunts these Fenlands. It began with the whispers that men went missing on the marshes – far more than is usual – and relentlessly the rumours grew, until the true horror became manifest. Now the assailant grows bolder. It comes with the dark and in the mists to bring terror and death, moving with great stealth to attack the villages and farms, to prey upon the unsuspecting, invading and murdering while the people sleep, bringing swift and terrible destruction. Then it is gone, vanished without trace into the night. It is no mere thief or raider, for it seems its only purpose is to kill with hideous brutality. The native men say it is not human. They claim it is a shadow walker – a *thyrs*. Perhaps you have heard of these horrors? Dark monstrous spirits that dwell in the depths of the swamps and are always thirsty for human blood. Belief in them is strong in these lands, and they are greatly dreaded.'

'Yes,' I said, feeling again with a shiver the full impact of my horrible experiences. 'I fear you are right that the fen-men remain pagans at heart. I have personally found cause to reprimand them for their crude superstitions.'

'Indeed?' He nodded and looked at me keenly as if to invite my further comment.

'Men who are afraid will imagine much,' I went on, intent on expressing my scorn for such foolish beliefs, even as I felt my sense of agitation rising. 'These marshes are dangerous, even to the locals who know them. They will quickly swallow a man without trace. It is natural for men to give monstrous forms to the common dangers which threaten them. Also the Fenlands are populated by outlaws and renegades, those cast out from human society, made vengeful and insane by their solitude and abandonment. I have seen how *in extremis* mere men may appear like monsters. I have also heard it said that occasionally there are men who conceal within them an insane desire to kill for the sake of killing. This murderer is surely only a man, but one possessed by such a fearsome madness… most likely by a demon.' I felt now a desperate need to believe in the truth of my own words, in those things which the Church had taught me, but once more my recollection of that huge, murderous and seemingly inhuman figure in the night rose into my mind to undermine all certainty and cast a chilling shadow of doubt deep within me.

'In fact,' Cadroc said, 'you are wrong, and the fen-men nearer to the truth. I must tell you that what stalks this land is not a man but truly a monster. A hellish thing emerged into our mortal world.'

'It cannot be so!' I said with shock. 'You are a monk of the Rule of St. Benedict. You surely do not believe in pagan tales of monsters?'

'This is not an earthly creature,' he answered, 'but a demon in corporeal form. I am a Briton, born in the wild forest-land of Elmet, and I can assure you I have good reason to know this. There are old and dreadful secrets in these lands which are known to we whose blood has dwelt here for many generations. The power of the Devil holds sway in these Fens. But I am versed in the ways of battling with the Evil One.' Grim-faced, he reached up to clasp the cross on his breast, as his other hand delved beneath the folds of his cloak to reveal a sword in a scabbard which hung from his belt, while he grasped the hilt firmly.

'You are the first monk I have known to carry a sword,' I said.

'I was not born a monk. In my youth I trained as a warrior. But now I have joined the war-band of Christ. I was raised in the kingdom of Elmet, in the tenets of the British Church. But I fled from my homeland years ago when the pagan barbarian King Penda invaded. Terrible days they were. Yes, indeed. Most terrible. It was later that I took the tonsure and converted to the Roman ways. When Lord Ecbehrt in desperation sent word to my abbot Botwulf, requesting the services of an exorcist to rid his land of this curse, my knowledge and experience ensured my appointment to the task. Ecbehrt is a Christian convert who deplores the stubbornness and backward ways of his own people. So you see that also there exists here a great opportunity for the Church against the vile sacrilege of paganism – the earthly hand of Satan. For now the people cower with fear inside their villages and pray to their devil-gods to protect them. When I overcome this monster, who will then be able to deny the supremacy of Christ over the heathen gods which have failed them?'

'You are hunting this murderer alone?' I said in disbelief. 'But how can you ever hope to track him down in this great wilderness?'

'My mission is ordained by God!' he answered simply. 'Yet there is more. I have followed the demon's trail from the Isle of Elge, to the south. Always it heads northward, as it visits its wrath and destruction upon the isolated settlements. Further to the north lie the deepest and darkest regions of the Fens, the lair from which I am convinced the horror has risen, and where I am sure it will seek to return. The northern settlements are remote and few, but this dark one's rage will not spare them, and once there I will close upon this devil and run it to ground. I will pursue it to the gates of Hell if I must.' Once more his face grew hard as he nodded gravely. Then he said: 'But it should not surprise us, we men of the Church, that such horrors occur at this time. Consider the year we are living in. "Let him who has comprehension reckon the number of the Beast: its number is six hundred and sixty-six." *Tempus Bestiam* – the time of the Beast. It is most surely a portent, a foreshadowing of the time to come: the Last Days, when Satan himself will break free from the eternal abyss.'

I shook my head. In my present state of mind I did not wish to discuss with him the fearful book of St. John's Revelation.

'The prophecy also reads: "It is the number of a man",' I observed. 'What if I am right, and you find this demon to learn that he is only a savage madman? How will your words of exorcism protect you from a mortal murderer?'

He frowned at me as if I were mocking him, then replied:

'Do not doubt that I have knowledge in these matters.' He reached inside his robe and produced a small hide-bound book which he opened before me, and I saw upon its pages grotesque diagrams of demonic figures and writings in a text I did not recognise – presumably some form of Celtic. 'As I have said, knowledge *and* experience.' Then he turned to point back in the direction from which we had come, saying: 'I have given you the explanation you asked for. It is time for you to return safely home. No doubt our arrival has disturbed the routine of your daily devotions. Farewell.'

So he dismissed me, and now it seemed that his words mocked me. I looked back to the remote woodland where my dwelling stood, realising suddenly how far away from it we had come. Yet the distant sight of it as it lay bleakly beneath a cluster of dark heavy clouds felt at once overwhelmingly dismal and oppressive, as I recalled for the first time since awakening the burdensome duty I owed this day to Ailisa, and gloomily anticipated my future solitude and confinement here. A kind of mad panic seemed suddenly to descend on me. I grew breathless while a cold sweat covered my body as I felt simply that I could no longer endure the misery of my situation. What Cadroc had implied seemed utterly true: of what use was I to anyone, alone and raving day after day in my cell as I slipped ever further towards madness? How could this achieve the redemption of my soul? Then, in that instant, as if with the force of divine inspiration, it seemed I understood with total clarity the meaning of it all, and I knew at once with certainty what it was I must do. With no time to consider further, I spun about and raced after the two men as they moved away.

'Brother, wait!' I called out. 'Forgive me if I appeared to doubt you.' Cadroc waved his hand at me as if to brush the matter aside, but I went on: 'I have indeed remembered something more, to reconcile our opinions. Whether this marauder is a man possessed by a demon, or truly a devil in the flesh, I must accept that it is an unholy creature. When I fled the scene of slaughter I sensed its presence come after me. In terror I cried out with holy words, and when I looked back it was gone. This is surely the reason that I alone have survived such an attack?' In fact I could not be sure of this – my feeling that I had been stalked by the killer as I fled from the massacre might simply have been born of my delirium and dread – but it seemed expedient now to say it, and indeed in that moment it felt like the truth to me. Cadroc gave a slight nod to indicate that I told him only that of which he was already certain. As he went to move on, my own purpose was becoming ever clearer, and as I continued to speak I reached out to grip his arm and detain him. 'Brother Cadroc, your fortitude and zeal have inspired me. There is more I must tell you. In the night I had a dream. And in this dream the evil thing from the fen came to me and we fought a great battle. It all seemed vivid and real and most terrifying, but I see now it was a sign and an injunction I dare not ignore. I awoke from this dream to find you at my bedside, then discovered that you are a godly man set upon a quest to fight with darkness itself.' I paused for a moment as I gathered courage to say now what I knew I must. 'I would go with you to confront the darkness. To do battle with the Devil. I see now it is what God demands of me.'

Cadroc's eyes bulged at me in a look of astonishment, then his expression turned to one of scorn.

'Go back to your refuge, Brother,' he answered. 'And the secure drudgery of your lonely prayers. You do not have the look of a holy warrior to me.'

'We are all the warriors of Christ!' I protested. 'I can assist you... I can be of service.'

'Your ardour is admirable. But I fear I have failed to impress upon you the great danger...'

'I understand, yet I believe the danger is sent to test me – to prove my faith. That it is sent by God in answer to my prayers.' Now I fell to my knees before him, as if I would make my confession, and the words poured from me in a frantic whisper. 'The darkness is always with me. I am in torment because I do not know finally if I am a man of God or else one of the wretched damned. I only know that *I do not know!* And I came out here alone so that I might cast this pernicious doubt from my heart, but shadow-like it eludes me and defeats me, driving me forever back into hopelessness and despair. But now my darkness has become a thing of solid form, an enemy I may pursue and fight and – with God's help and yours – overcome. You, Brother, are too resolute in your faith to understand this – a thing that fills me with the sinful impulse of envy – yet I hope that within you pity may take the place of understanding. I beg you to grant me what I ask.'

His dark eyes studied me closely for long moments, and I believed that beneath his stern look I saw something there to encourage me – some sign of inner hesitation or uncertainty. But this was only momentary, before he turned from me, saying:

'Go home, Brother. Mine is not a pleasant pilgrimage. I have no place for passengers.'

He strode off after his companion, and I stood dejectedly as I watched him depart. But my heart was filled at once with the overpowering conviction that my words were absolute truth, and with sudden unshakeable determination I started to follow them.

Chapter Eight

We walked throughout the morning, and I followed precisely their arduous path through the mud and bulrushes as we circled the borders of the deeper marshes where men dare not tread, while a thin mist rose up, making it difficult for me to mark time. Occasionally Cadroc would look around and I heard his voice boom out over the open wetlands, commanding me to turn back, yet I kept moving doggedly onward, keeping them always in my sight. After a time I began to study my surroundings: the eerie, silent miles of dull grey reeds and steaming swamps. We encountered not another soul as we went, and I was struck once more by the sheer size and emptiness of this land, whose twisting tortuous pathways might turn the journey of an hour into a day and where a man feels he is led ever farther from the sight of God. It chilled me to my bones.

It was probably around noon that I felt the ground sink as I followed them into a kind of hollow, and the mist grew thicker as it swirled up to surround us. Soon I saw that a wide lake stretched before us. We skirted its edge, until a small collection of rotting huts appeared up ahead. As Cadroc and Aelfric approached them I saw dimly that an old man sat outside the door to one of these, his attention fixed upon the repair of a fishing net.

'Greetings,' Aelfric called to him. 'We come here in peace.'

Suddenly aware of their presence, the old fellow cried out in fear and jumped to his feet, snatching up a spear from the ground beside him, straining with rheumy eyes to peer at them through the mist as he began to yell out at the top of his voice.

'Good man, be calm,' I heard Cadroc say. 'Be assured that we mean you no harm.' But the old man continued with his caterwauling, shouting out desperate threats as his spear remained defiantly raised. Then another, younger man appeared behind him, his own spear pointed at them, and he too began to yell and bluster, excited by the older man's panic. Now Cadroc's voice thundered out at them.

'Fools! We are here upon God's work. Do not dare to obstruct us, or you will suffer His wrath!' He stepped forward and raised his arm, his finger pointing at them, then he swept it down in a masterful gesture as he cried out: 'Lay down your spears!'

Their weapons fell to the ground, as if forcibly torn from their hands, and they quailed visibly before Cadroc's words, until the younger one fell to his knees and I heard him hiss:

'Father! Be still. It is Aelfric. He comes with a holy man! Forgive father,' he implored. 'He is old… your coming alarmed him… his sight and hearing are poor… he did not recognise you in the mist. You come to us in bad times. There is much fear everywhere.'

'That is all right, Alfhere,' Aelfric said cheerfully, and clapped a hand onto his shoulder. 'Now get up. We need you to take us across the water.'

'Of course, of course,' Alfhere nodded eagerly. 'But first you will eat and drink with us?'

'No time,' Aelfric shook his head. 'Our mission is urgent.'

'Then come,' Alfhere replied. I approached as he led the others along the lake's shore to where a coracle lay upon the mud. And as he dragged it into the water I knew with a sense of desperation that we had reached the point where I could follow Cadroc no further, and that I would be left here, many perilous miles from home, stranded in this desolate, hostile place. I moved to the side of the boat, waiting silently as Cadroc and Aelfric clambered into it, my gaze simply fixed upon them. Alfhere, assuming me to be their companion, looked up at me and said: 'Do you seek passage?'

I did not answer him but only looked to Brother Cadroc. His eyes would not meet mine, but now Aelfric shot me an angry stare, which in moments changed into a look of amusement; then he began to laugh as he whispered something to Cadroc. Now the monk turned to glare at me indignantly, but I must have looked like the proverbial lost lamb, as once more I received the impression that something within the man was uncertain and divided, for after a moment his anger subsided, and he appeared to relent.

'Come then,' he said, and shifted to make a space in the boat beside him. 'For now, at least.'

'Thank you, truly,' I said to him as I climbed in, feeling a flood of incredible relief.

'And I say truly that you should not thank me,' he muttered. 'You would be safer abandoned on the marsh, Brother.'

But I also turned to give Aelfric my thanks, for I felt his words to Cadroc had perhaps been instrumental in my acceptance into their company. In that moment I came to regard Aelfric as a friend.

As Alfhere rowed us over the lake, and I felt the sudden exhilaration of freedom and the cool wet breeze on my face, it came to me that by embarking on this voyage across the water I had passed over a boundary from which I could not turn back. Whatever might lie ahead, it had now become my fixed path into a strange and mysterious world of darkness and great danger. But I was convinced that here burned the fire that would temper my soul: a chance to serve as a companion and perhaps even an apprentice to an exorcist monk and learn the secret ways of battling with the Dark One. I prayed my courage would prove equal to the task. But then I thought of Ailisa, and I questioned whether what had prompted my actions was courage at all. I wondered if, in my coward's heart, I might have run away anywhere to escape my responsibility to her, to place some distance between us and make our parting easier.

When we had crossed the lake, to the point where the beds of reeds grew too thick for the coracle to go further, we climbed ashore, and Aelfric said:

'Now we must continue north. This will bring us to the settlement called Meretun where we will find welcome and lodging tonight.'

We walked for hours on snaking pathways across a series of small islets which rose and fell out of the marshes, following tracks over thin ridges of firm ground which formed a connection of narrow causeways between them, while gulls soared and cried above us. But all else was deathly quiet and still except for the wails and shrieks of the marsh birds which sometimes rose, like the unearthly sobbing of lost damned souls upon the sharp salt winds that blew in from the distant sea and merged with the pervading stench of rotting slime, which drifted everywhere in clouds of vapour from out of the oozing depths of the mud. At first Cadroc did not speak but only trudged onward as his eyes held a faraway look, which made it seem that as he travelled he simultaneously traversed some inward realm of his own, and I sensed how heavily the burden of his responsibility must lay upon him. Eventually I began to converse quietly with Aelfric as he strode in front and held his spear, pausing occasionally to test with the blunt end of its wooden shaft the firmness of the ground ahead, saying to him:

'Are you not afraid to journey through the fens on the trail of this killer?'

He smiled and raised his spear with both hands as he answered.

'I do not fear. The Fenland is my home. And life spent in fear is no life.'

'But you must have confidence in Brother Cadroc's powers. Are you a Christian man?'

'I have made worship to the Christ-god,' he said briefly. I understood his meaning. Most of the fen-men respected our faith, but to them the Christian god remained only one among many. As Cadroc had confided to me, it was by his mission here that he intended to change that situation. But it was also clear to me that he had other motivations beyond this, and these I determined to discover.

My thoughts distracted me, and my muscles had grown tired and aching from my long travail. It was now, as I followed Aelfric down an uneven slope from an islet onto the marsh, that I lost my footing and tripped, then lurched to one side, stumbling away from our path. The ground there looked firm, and no different to me from where I had walked before, but as I stepped onto it my legs sank instantly down to my knees in soft viscous mud. I shifted my weight and fell onto my backside to stop myself from sinking further, then slipped and scrabbled as I tried to free myself, but my hands found nothing solid to grip beneath me, and a sense of panic came over me as I realised I was hopelessly stuck.

'Keep still!' Aelfric called out, as he began to approach me, making his way forward with infinite care. Then he lay down flat on his stomach, stretching out across the ground behind me to spread his weight there evenly, and reached out his arm towards me. Slowly I twisted around to clutch at his outstretched hand, but my own fingers were slippery with mud and at first I could not gain a firm grip. Finally we managed to grasp each other about our wrists, then I clung to him with both hands as he began to crawl backwards, pulling me with him while I squirmed and kicked, my body sweating with fear and exertion until slowly I felt myself torn loose from the mire's deadly grip. Then a loud squelching noise came out from the mud, as if it protested to be robbed of its prey.

As I clambered to my feet, Aelfric stood before me, his look at once growing hard and stern as he told me:

'You must be watchful. The marsh is always hungry for those who are not wary. This time you are lucky, but next time...' and at once his face broke into its customary grin as he slapped my arm '...you might lose your boots!'

'Indeed we must be vigilant!' Cadroc spoke to me now, his voice like gravel in his throat and his eyes sharp with warning. 'Death surrounds us on every side. It is truly said that the right path that leads to life is narrow and hard, yet many and wide are the wrong paths that lead to suffering and darkness.'

'I will be careful, I promise,' I said, feeling a stab of fear as I nodded to show him that I understood his meaning: of things deeper and more terrible still than the black quagmires of the Fens. But now it occurred to me how absurdly ill-matched my two companions were: one forever smiling and good-humoured, the other so relentlessly grim, as if between them they stood to represent the opposite extremes of human nature. In other circumstances their partnership might have seemed almost comical. Yet upon that journey, as I studied Aelfric in unguarded moments when his thoughts were silent and his face grew still, I began to sense that perhaps his good-nature was an affectation which served him as a mask, or as a defence against the world, and I wondered if a different man existed beneath it.

Now that my misadventure had roused Cadroc from his silent musings, I took the opportunity to speak with him.

'I thank you again,' I said respectfully, 'for allowing me to join you. May I ask what it was that changed your mind?'

'I have been debating that matter to myself,' he replied. 'Your words outside your hermitage have remained in my thoughts. I find myself wondering if there is any truth in what you say, and whether indeed some divine purpose might accompany you. But I may come to decide otherwise' – his brow grew furrowed for a moment – 'in which case I will arrange to send you back. For the time being your show of great determination has impressed me.'

'I remember your own words,' I said, 'which implied some secret knowledge of the enemy's true nature. Will you tell me this story?'

He considered for a moment, then nodded.

'Indeed I will tell you both. It is well you should know it. In my homeland, when I was a very young man, in the days before King Penda invaded but after the Britons under King Cadwallon had liberated Elmet from the overlordship of the Northern Angles, the rule there had reverted to the native British lords, of whom my father was one. At this time the peasants who lived on the edge of the forest came to us to say that the dark spirits who dwelt in the forest's depths had begun to emerge to plague their homes. These were not mortal creatures, they claimed, not men but monsters led by the Devil, for his form might be seen in the shadows among them, bigger and greater than all the rest. Before this, they explained, they had dutifully said their prayers and hung the symbol of the Cross inside their huts. Until now this had always kept the dark ones at bay. But no longer. Now they came at night with inhuman howls and cries, attacking and killing and driving men to flee from their homes. And when the men returned in the daylight, they found their dwellings ravaged, their possessions destroyed and their stocks of food stolen. Soon they would starve, they cried, and even the Holy Cross no longer had the power to protect them. My father listened to their ravings doubtfully and concluded that a pack of bandits must be hiding out in the forest. He sent men to search there, but no trace could be found of a large outlaw presence, only the usual motley collection of a few thieves and cut-throats, who were duly rounded up and executed. But still the attacks in the night continued.

'This situation went on until our land lived in a state of constant terror, but the cause of it remained unknown, and my father was at a loss to know what to do. Then one day the captain of the guards came to him to report that he had captured a wild man from the forest, who remarkably had come to surrender himself and was now imprisoned in the dungeon of our fortress. Yet our captain said this creature had carried with him a fine sword and seemed to be something other than a mere savage. I went with my father to investigate, and we came upon a fearsome-looking figure of great height and size. At first in my shock I thought we had captured the Devil himself. But he stood before us, presenting himself in a way that suggested dignity and breeding. And as I inspected him I saw his body and limbs were perfectly in human proportion and that beneath

his raggedness his face seemed both intelligent and attra
Now he spoke in what we recognised to be the Anglish to
– it was before I became conversant in your speech – but in my
father's service was a man who had some understanding of the
language, who was summoned to act as our interpreter.

'The story we heard was therefore necessarily brief and
simple. The stranger claimed he had discovered, deep in the
forest, the existence of a secret lair of devils. He would lead
us there, he said, if we swore oaths that we would return his
sword to him, that he should go in the vanguard of our attack
and that the life of the chief devil was to be his alone.

'My father and I went away to discuss his proposal. We
knew we must take this chance to rid our land of its curse,
but if the accounts we had been given were true – if what we
faced were really devils – then we doubted our power as men
to overcome them. We would need spiritual help. So we went
to our local community of monks to seek advice.

'The monks took us into the presence of the oldest man
in their order, a man named Brother Albinus. When he heard
our words, he threw up his hands to the heavens and appeared
transported with joy.

' "Throughout my life," he said, "I have been tormented
many times by an evil dream, a portent of damnation which
is God's punishment for a great sin committed in my youth.
But when I was a boy, I once heard it said that deep in the
forest lies a secret cave known to be an entrance into the
underworld. It is a place once sacred to the ancient priesthood
called the Druids, who long ago fled there seeking sanctuary
from the proscription against them by the old Romans. Here
they conjured dark magic filled with hatred and vengeance
against their foreign persecutors until they opened up a mouth
into Hell itself. But their sorcery was so powerful and dreadful

it entirely consumed them, driving them to degradation and madness, and making them into demonic spirits, half men and half beasts forever bound to this world by their eternal thirst for revenge. In my dream I am taken by night into this place, and I wander through the cavernous darkness to the gates of Hell, hearing beyond me the groans and cries of many damned souls until I fear I will die of fright and join them. Always I awaken in a state of horror and hurry to my devotions, forever dreading that the next night will be my last. But now you have made it clear to me that God offers me my chance of redemption. It is a sign which tells me to go out and lift this curse from our land; and this will be to lift the threat of damnation from my own head. Ask your stranger if the lair of these devils lies inside a cave. If it is so, then we will go with you, for we know a rite of exorcism which will seal these foul spirits forever inside the earth."

'The stranger confirmed to us that the devils' den was indeed situated within a hidden cave. So it was that one morning, before dawn, I set out with my father and our men, and many staunch peasants who went with us along with Brother Albinus, his monks, and the giant stranger who would act as our guide. We returned his sword to him, and we carried our own swords, which had been blessed by the monks with holy charms, while the peasants came armed with spears, knives and clubs, and carried torches to light our way through the darkness.

'We journeyed for more than half the day, the stranger following signs he had left carved upon trees along the way. He grew more agitated, and made signals with his hands to urge us on with greater speed – I presumed to reach and surprise the devils in the daytime when their powers were weakest.

'The sun had sunk far beyond its high point when we came

to a place above a valley between two high hills with giant rugged stones which jutted out from under the grass and bushes on their steep slopes, and I looked down upon a great round bubble of rock which lay deep in the valley itself. I remember it now as clearly as if I saw it this day. Also I remember the sinking feeling deep in my stomach as my excitement turned to apprehension when I saw the stranger point towards it and say something in a tone I knew to mean that we had come to our destination.

'First my father and the stranger went stealthily by themselves to examine the ground about the base of the bulbous rock, and soon they found concealed there in the scrub the narrow crevice that would lead us to the gates of Hell. They signalled to us, and we re-lit our torches then crept to join them, gathering together about the rock in our full numbers. Now my father came to me and told me to gather my courage, saying we must go at the front to set an example to the others. I steeled my nerves as I followed him and the stranger down into the icy darkness, and behind us filed the monks along with the best and bravest of our warriors. We moved along a cold, dank passageway, the light from our torches barely penetrating the intense blackness, until we emerged into what seemed like a wide cavern, and I could tell from the direction of our movements that it must be located inside the highest hill itself. At our feet lay the entrance to another passage which seemed to lead downwards, deep into the ground, and since we had encountered nothing so far, I supposed the devils must lay concealed in this. But I felt a thrill of pure horror as I saw that scattered about us were many gnawed and discarded bones, from which I turned my eyes in fear I should recognise them as human remains.

'Now the monks came forward, and began to chant. It was a

terrible yet glorious sound, an unworldly cacophony of prayers and curses which rang in the air, echoing and reverberating through the great walls of stone until it filled the depths of the earth beneath us. Then there came suddenly a great thundering from under our feet as the ground itself began to shake, and the air was clogged with a foul-smelling haze which rose to blind our eyes and burn our throats as we stood blinking into the shadows. And at once all in front of us was alive, light and dark and dust swirling together into frantic motion as a hellish swarm of utterly demonic faces rose up at us. Hideous they were as they rushed upon us, their distorted inhuman features twisted and screaming, and we thrust out our swords in terror to hold back these legions of Hell. But then in their midst, through the clouds of dust, there materialised a face that was a brutish parody of the human form, a gigantic vision that rose and towered above us. Its body, half-concealed in the haze, appeared naked and horribly misshapen as its eyes burned with savage rage, and it bared its fangs to roar at us. We who were mere men shrank back, so terrifying was this manifestation, and we feared it was a horror no mortal could fight. But the monks held fast, frail old Albinus to the fore, thrusting up their wooden crosses into the demon's face, forcing it back as it bellowed out once more, and the holy men closed upon it as they shrieked out their frantic imprecations.

'Now there was a tremendous rumbling from all around, and the earth itself seemed to shudder. Then the cave was collapsing about us, giant lumps of stone tumbling from above, falling down to crush and bury those detestable spirits. But even in the midst of this, I saw the stranger leap forward, fighting his way through the crowd of fleeing monks, heedless of the danger, with his sword poised ready to strike as he came before that monstrous giant demon. Yet I saw him pause, in the midst of all this pandemonium, and stare deep into its eyes before he drove his blade forward, thrusting it hard into the devil's black heart. And as he struck the fiend was simply gone, vanished back into the darkness and crashing chaos from which it had arisen.

'All of us turned now and fled, hurtling blindly back towards the outside world. As we emerged out into the blessed daylight, the great thundering from beneath us grew louder than ever as clouds of noxious black smoke came billowing out from the cave entrance. Some of our men were lost, but I saw the stranger emerge, his face and body streaked with grime.

'I collapsed onto the ground, and others fell beside me, coughing and fighting for breath, also gasping in fear at what we had seen. When I regained some part of my senses I rose and slowly recovered myself, and later I looked for the stranger, but he was gone. No one had seen him leave. And I never saw him again.

'After this, the wicked attacks on our population ceased. We sealed the cave entrance with giant rocks, to be sure that nothing from inside might ever find its way back into the world of men. And Brother Albinus was never again troubled by his night terrors, knowing at last he had been absolved of his sin. You will now understand, Brother Athwold, why I have agreed to your presence here. How your words to me of omens, dreams and damnation seemed like an echo from the distant past. I would not deny a man his right to seek salvation. The story I have told was also the beginning of my own true devotion to Christ, for I had seen with my own eyes the spells of His monks defeat devils and bring down in ruins the very temple of Satan. In the book I carry are transcribed the words of those monks' age-old rituals, and armed with them I have come to rid this Fenland of its same curse.'

As Cadroc concluded his account, told with such conviction that I dared not doubt it, my head was spinning. As I journeyed deeper into these pagan lands all I had ever believed was starting to unravel in my mind as I reflected that perhaps the world held greater mysteries than I – and the Church – had been prepared to admit. It seemed that deep and ancient feelings were stirring in my soul, uncertainties I could not define, but which grew stronger with each step I took, becoming one with the unremitting gloom which surrounded us.

We had come to a place of higher ground, thick with trees; and it was as we made our way through this stretch of woodland that we entered suddenly into a clearing. And I saw something which sent a burst of shock spreading through me. There in front, hanging by its neck from the low branch of a sturdy ash tree, was the body of a man – clearly an executed outlaw. A great hulking horror he must have been in life, raggedly dressed and caked in mud and filth. And now the body had begun to rot.

'Ah! Civilisation!' Aelfric beamed. 'We are nearly there.'

I gazed transfixed at the horrible sight. The body appeared quite terrifying, even in death, with its eyes picked out by the scavengers. Like the ravaged corpses I had found beyond my hermitage, it seemed to me that this brutish-looking thing could never truly have been human. Then I saw that in the tree, directly above the corpse, there perched a large crow. My blood grew cold, for the whole scene, suddenly encountered, appeared somehow portentous and uncanny. The bird looked directly down at me, its eyes gleaming as it began to caw loudly. I grew rigid, for the sight and sound of it took me backwards in time to the days of my childhood when my grandmother, a woman of the old religion, would explain to me and my siblings that crows were the messengers of the gods. And she, a person of gentle nature, would become uncharacteristically strict whenever a crow would call, and demand we children should fall silent and listen.

This thought brought other distant memories flooding into my mind, so colourful and vivid that they felt for a fleeting moment almost tangible and real, as it seemed I was returned to my family homeland in Middle Anglia, to the days of my infancy when my kin would gather with all those who lived and worked on our estate to celebrate the ancient festivals of midsummer and yule, of the harvest time, and of the spring goddess Eostra – she of the shining dawn. I almost felt that I sat once more upon my father's shoulders to look out across our fields and see the priests of the old faith clad in bright flowing robes, performing rituals to the sun and to the spirits of nature who would bring fertility to our soil. Sometimes the villagers would dress in strange costumes to enact mock battles, where they drove back into the outer darkness a villainous masked figure clad in black who was the symbol of cruel winter, whose appearance would always thrill and delight me. In my childish innocence these had seemed like events of wonder and joy, of feasting and singing, dancing and laughter: a magical joining together of everyone in our community. I could not deny they were happy memories. It was soon after this that the Christian monks came – first Irish and then Roman – to bring the light of Truth, and show us that in our simplicity we had all been as children who had not understood the true meaning of religion and life.

As I stared up at the crow I felt Aelfric's eyes upon me, and then I saw him grin with mischievous amusement.

'It seems,' he said, 'that Christians are so eager to abandon the old beliefs, but the old ways are not yet ready to abandon them.'

At once I felt foolish and ashamed. I glanced back over my shoulder at the hanging corpse to reassure myself firmly it was only a man and all that had seemed uncanny about it was simply in my own mind. Then I went quickly onward.

Chapter Nine

At last we approached the place called Meretun. In keeping with its name – the village by the mere – it stood close to a wide stretch of water, and was large by the standards of a Fenland settlement, although it would not have been considered so in any other land. Aelfric began to call out as we drew near, to announce our presence and avoid causing alarm, and soon a band of men gathered at the village entrance to meet us. On the outskirts we passed by a rough wooden shrine, old and weather-beaten, which housed a vividly carved idol of the pagan god Thunor, who sat growling at us as he clutched to his breast his great war hammer. As we entered the men exchanged greetings of friendly familiarity with Aelfric, who asked them:

'What news?'

'A party of our men went out yesterday on a fowling expedition,' answered one in a subdued tone. 'They do not yet come back.'

Aelfric hissed between clenched teeth, then said:

'We have come here from the Crowland, where last night there was a new attack.'

'Ahh!' the other man's face assumed a look of horror. 'This devil travels fast. He does not go on human feet.'

'You cannot be sure of that, Gyrth,' Aelfric said. 'Your men may yet return. But I bring this man, who is called Brother Cadroc, sent by our ealdorman to combat with Christian magic this great evil which threatens us.'

All eyes were turned warily upon Cadroc and me, their disparate looks suddenly concentrated into one of single intensity. And I sensed then the great fear which hung like a miasma over this village, along with the clear impression that our arrival inspired them with little hope. It was Cadroc's sworn duty to win over such people as these.

Aelfric now turned to me and pointed towards a building which stood on the far side of the village, the largest structure in the whole settlement.

'I must go with Brother Cadroc to present him to the headman and village elders,' he said. 'You must go to the village hall, where we will eat and sleep tonight. We will join you later.'

I left them, but instead of going straight to the hall I began to wander about the village. I sought to reacquaint myself with the noises and smells of a human settlement, which had recently grown unfamiliar to me. I walked beyond the village centre to where women worked at the looms in the weaving-house and men laboured with mallets and chisels to cut wood to turn and shape on their lathes. Then I came to a cluster of small dwellings where the air was thick with smoke and the rich odours of cooking. Wives peered out at me through open doors as they crouched over their steaming cauldrons in the shadows, and muddy children froze in the midst of their noisy games to gape at me as I went past. Finally I came upon a small crowd of people who stood gathered outside an isolated hut.

Others were now deserting their occupations to hurry over and join them, and becoming curious I went and stood among them to see what was happening there. Standing inside I saw a man of most remarkable appearance. Tall and spare, his features sharp and somehow striking, he wore a long grey cloak over a robe of dark blue into which there were embroidered tufts of fur from different animals and patterns made from many small pieces of jewel-like crystal which glittered and sparkled as he moved. He held a staff that was almost as tall as he was. It was made out of gnarled elm and carved into a thick knob at the top and decorated along the sides with strips of polished brass that were marked their entire length with elaborate runic symbols. Yet he seemed to handle this cumbersome object with great ease and dexterity. On the floor near to his feet lay a wide-brimmed hat adorned with raven feathers, and I knew this to signify that he was an adept of Woden, the pagan god of sorcery and of the Brotherhood of Shamans. This man was a heathen wizard. Such people were reckoned among those of the old faith to be skilful healers, and at present it was clear he was in the midst of a healing ritual.

Before him an injured man lay upon a rug spread across the floor. His forearm was stretched out to expose a deep, ugly gash which was bleeding badly. A strip of cloth had been tied tightly about his upper arm to restrict the flow of blood, and the man lay still and seemed to be overcome with shock. A fire burned in the hearth, and thick smoke filled the interior of the bare hut. As the shaman leaned over the man his arms were outstretched and his cloak swished about him in the growing swirls of smoke, which weaved their drifting patterns into the darkness while he appeared in their midst to become a figure of awesome and almost superhuman power. He was uttering incantations in a tone that was intense and utterly commanding.

> 'I entreat the great ones, keepers of the heavens,
> Earth I ask, and sky, and the gods' high hall,
> And the fair holy goddess, to grant this gift of healing.'

As he chanted the air itself was thick with the sense of something deep and powerful; and the wounded man seemed to be sinking into a state that was like sleep, except that his eyes remained open; yet they appeared blank and unseeing, and it occurred to me now that the shaman must have cast some kind of enchantment over him. As I glanced at those crowded about me it appeared they too were caught in the shaman's spell, gazing motionless and nearly trance-like at the proceedings until it began to feel as if their minds were almost joined together in a state of collective awareness. At once it came to me that it was not proper for a Christian monk to attend and be a witness to these things within a pagan place of worship, and I tried to turn and depart. But more of the villagers had now come to stand behind me and I found myself caught up in the press of the crowd. And in truth I felt a sudden sense of curiosity at what I was observing. Now the shaman spoke to the spellbound man.

'Beorna, son of Leofric, a spirit of sickness would enter into you, and all here must join together to cast it out.' He brought his hand to rest very close to the sick man's face, his fingers moving in slow and undulating motions, and the man's eyes fell shut as the shaman began to intone another charm.

> 'Spirits of Air will carry you,
> Upon the falcon's wing,
> Under the eagle's claw,

> To the sky god's realm,
> Where pain is no more,
> And the body forgotten.
> Let your soul bathe there in light,
> Until this work is done.'

Now his breathing began to rise and fall in perfect time with that of the injured man, creating the strong sense of a visible link between them as together they appeared to sink deeper into a state of entrancement.

Suddenly the shaman cast away his staff and fell to his knees, reaching out to clamp his hand about the man's wrist, and he seemed then to become locked in a great inward struggle as his breathing came in shuddering gasps and sweat broke from his brow. He muttered more incantations deep in his throat, his voice at first a growl I could barely understand, and his eyes grew unfocused as his tone rose louder and clearer.

> 'I summon you, venomous one,
> I call you out from blood, flesh and bone.
> Shrivel like kindling on the hearth,
> Shrink like water in the pail,
> Fade like dung upon the earth.
> I cast you beyond,
> Out into the darkness,
> Out into the death-lands,
> To the place of your exile.'

I was becoming alarmed by the sheer intensity of these things when suddenly the eyes of the afflicted man opened and appeared to change. From within their blankness there emerged an expression of wild alertness as they darted from side to side, while his body began to shiver violently. Yet his state did not seem like a natural one but rather a condition of fevered delirium as his breath rose and fell in harsh gulps, and then he rasped out in a tone that sounded full of dread. His words were incomprehensible, but his voice seemed incredibly to pass into and then emerge clearly out of the mouth of the shaman himself.

'I see it! The darkness is before me… its image rises like a shadow… dimly reflected… in the eyes of another!' As the shaman cried out these words his own features twisted sharply. I felt fear spread palpably into the crowd about me. But also I felt it within myself, growing like a contagion, as at once it seemed that these words came from somewhere beyond both the sick man and the shaman – that something terrible and unnatural had begun to happen, and the situation was fast spiralling out of control. Sensing this, the shaman fought to regain command and increased his efforts, seizing the groaning man's head with both hands. 'Be at peace!' he demanded. 'What would invade your body is tormenting your mind. Cast it from within you and be at peace. I order you, unclean spirit, to be gone!'

The struggle went on, fearful in its escalating intensity, while I could feel those around me swaying and jerking with every motion the shaman made. Then I felt myself moving with them, all of us drawn in by what we were witnessing until it felt as if all our bodies moved as one. The sick man had fallen back into his trance, and finally the shaman raised his head, his eyes rolling, his body soaked with sweat as he pulled his hand free and thrust it out, gesturing up into the gloom overhead.

'See!' he called. 'The corruption is cast out. It has fled!'

All of us looked upward in a single movement, and those around me gasped out, as if they saw something in the shadows about the rafters. At first I saw nothing, but as I looked harder it seemed I began to discern there a vague shape which was like a cloud of pure black vapour that found form against the lesser darkness, beginning to swirl and spread like blood spilt into water. I stood overcome by what I supposed I saw, and my heart grew cold. Then my eyes closed as if I sought involuntarily to shut out the sight of it. But this gave me no escape as I seemed to feel the nebulous image enter into my head, as if it came to invade my inner senses. And still, in my mind's eye, those threads of darkness twisted before me until I saw at last that they grew paler, then became as clouds of steam that drifted into the night air. From beyond them there came a sound of faint growling breaths that rose and fell, as at once my inward sight found clarity and I watched it approach – the shadow-shrouded thing from out on the fen. And in a single chilling instant I understood that the memory of it was rising within me.

Still I could not see its face, but as it drew closer I began to make out its form, huge and distorted as it loomed over me, brutish and utterly horrible, with long hair that straggled from what looked like the outline of a grossly misshapen head. I knew then with certainty that it could be nothing human. It was all that my darkest imaginings might suppose to be monstrous. And within moments I knew the full horror of it would be revealed to me – a sight I could not bear to face.

I gave a small gasp as my eyes burst open, and the image was dispelled. But even as this happened the glazed eyes of the shaman found instant sharpness and focus as his head jerked upward and his gaze met mine with a piercing intensity. I felt a great tremor of shock pass through me with the sensing of some deep and instantaneous connection between us. Vaguely I watched him return to the motionless form before him, but now I looked upon his actions only distantly, for my mind was left shaken and numb.

I looked back at the stricken man's wound, as the shaman went over to the hearth, snatching something from out of the fire, and I saw then it was a bone-handled knife, the metal blade burning hot as he held it up before us, waving it in slow circular motions while he called out:

'Spirit of Fire, I call upon you to burn the fortress of this poisonous one so that he may not return to it.'

He knelt and laid the blade upon the deep wound, as the smell of scorched flesh filled the air, and remarkably the gash appeared to become closed by the heat as the bleeding was staunched. But throughout this the sick man incredibly gave no sign of awareness or pain, and did not stir. Next the shaman reached for a leather bag which lay nearby and drew from it a pot which contained a type of salve. He scooped out some of this and smeared it over the injury, where it quickly seemed to congeal into something like a poultice. Then he called for strips of clean linen and bandaged them about the arm. Finally he instructed the man to return and awaken, and the shaman's spell seemed instantly to lift and break as the atmosphere in the hut grew light, and the people there began to stir and talk as if we had all woken together from a shared dream.

The villagers were dispersing, and as they went they gave their thanks and blessings to the shaman, whom they called Taeppa. As I turned to move away, my senses remained dazed. I felt I had foolishly allowed myself to become involved and absorbed in something that was wrong and perhaps even dangerous, and that I was still struggling to free my mind from its powerful influence. Then I felt a strong hand clamp onto my shoulder, and I looked around with a start to see once more the fierce eyes of the shaman fixed upon mine.

'Come with me!' he said abruptly, and pulled me with him back inside the hut, gesturing impatiently to those who had raised up the afflicted man to depart and leave us. He closed the door behind them, shutting us alone together in virtual darkness, except for the red glow of the dying firelight. Sweat covered his face, and he appeared exhausted from his exertions, but he was plainly determined to hold me there. My mind still felt shocked and half dazed, but I attempted to gain control of myself as I made to move back towards the door. I did not wish to speak with this man. But at once he stepped into my path to prevent my departure, then he demanded: 'What is it that you know?'

'I know nothing...' I stammered as I tried to find the strength to resist the strange power of his gaze, which seemed at once to hold me to the spot. 'Nothing I would say to a heathen sorcerer. I am a Christian monk. *Let me pass!*'

Now I flinched in fear as suddenly he drew up his bone-handled knife and brought it before my eyes, then he began to move it back and forth in a slow and rhythmic fashion. In spite of myself I found my stare fixed upon it with a fearful fascination which seemed to deprive me still further of my powers of conscious thought. Now his voice rose up, low yet commanding, as once more I felt the atmosphere in the hut grow heavy amidst all the smoke and gloom, and he began to speak another spell, or rather to chant it in a dreamy singsong tone, his extraordinary presence becoming overwhelming as his words seemed to draw my senses away from me, invading every part of my mind, like a whisper that was uttered far away while remaining very sharp and clear.

'Outward we go to the realm within,
There to walk and there to see.

Inward we go to the realm without,
To the land that lies beyond.'

As he recited this he slowly brought the flat of the knife's blade closer to my face, so near to my eyes that my vision blurred, and in my discomfort my eyelids began to close as he continued his chanting:

'As above, so below,
As without, so within.
Thus the charm is done.'

The echo of these confusing words seemed to resonate inside the hut, and my mind now felt so light and strange that it began to seem like I was no longer entirely within the living world. And when the shaman spoke again his voice sounded as if it were confined to the farthest borderland of my senses.

'Do not hide behind your dogmas. This is a matter of gravest importance. The land is in danger and I sense you have knowledge of this. You have seen… *something!* The spirits have declared it. The Fates have whispered it to me.'

'I do not believe in fate,' I objected weakly, 'but in the providence of God.'

'Call it what you will. By any name it is equally mysterious. Come now, and speak. Unburden your soul to me. I must know all.' His soft tone was silky and somehow sinister, gently cajoling, while I felt as if I stood upon the brink of a warm and embracing blackness. And the words broke from me before I could prevent it.

'I have seen the darkness,' I said, almost strangely relieved to make this confession, 'and looked into its face – the ravening monster which stalks this land. But my mind was fevered…

114

disordered. I cannot clearly remember what it was I saw.'

'Then we must restore the memory and give it clarity. Our bodily eyes may be deceived, but never the eyes of the soul – the true recorder of all experience. The reality of what you have seen lies deep within you, and we must know what it is your mind conceals like a cloud which blocks out the sun. You alone among the living have lain eyes on this evil one. It has placed its mark upon you, and you will not be freed until you find the courage to confront it. So you must seek it out. We must pursue the monster inside your mind, and from there into the world outside.'

'I cannot... cannot...' I heard myself gasp with sudden dread. 'I fear the darkness beyond all things. To commune with it is forbidden.'

'There is discord in you,' he whispered sharply. 'Much that is obscured and in disharmony. You must understand that you are not upon this earth to fear the judgement of God, or the condemnation of men, but to seek and discover the truth that is within you. This will bring light into your darkness.'

At once my body trembled and my scalp began to tingle as I felt an awesome sense of the profound and the unworldly. In some part of myself I felt wholly awake and alive. What powers of perception did this man possess, to see so clearly into my heart and mind? I knew in that moment a lightness of being that was like the freedom of the soul, as if my old self had become something distant and heavy, a burden to be cast off. It felt truly astounding and utterly enticing: a sense of untold possibility. But in the next instant there came a great crash, and I turned, startled and bewildered, to see there had burst through the door a figure whose face was a twisted vision of pure rage. It was several moments before my sight grew clear and I recognised it as Brother Cadroc.

'*Enough!*' he spat at the shaman, who bared his teeth and snarled back at Cadroc with thwarted fury. Cadroc strode to my side and grabbed at my robe, pulling me to the door as the shaman followed, and it felt to me as if an angel and a demon were fighting for my very soul. I stumbled out blinking into the light as the villagers who stood nearby looked on with astonishment. The shaman emerged from the hut, standing at the door as he glared at Cadroc and said:

'How dare you violate this venerated place. Would you challenge me, monk?'

'No indeed,' Cadroc answered with studied disdain. 'I have a greater battle to fight, and my actions will prove my powers.' Then he turned to address the villagers. 'This wizard might make a fine show of fighting petty devils, but be aware that I have come to contend with a great one. With Christian prayers I will cast it from the earth, back down into Hell, as a surgeon cuts an arrowhead from the living flesh. Victory will show mine to be the true God.'

The villagers seemed much impressed by this claim, perhaps expecting a contest to develop between shaman and monk – between the old magic and the new. Now the shaman turned his gaze upon me, looking deep into my eyes as he pointed a finger at me and said:

'You must return to me, to finish what has been started.'

In my confused state I felt an overpowering and involuntary urge to obey. I think it was only the ferocious look in Cadroc's eyes that brought me to myself, as in horror I began to understand how subtly and deeply this sorcerer had imposed his will upon me: his guileful influence seeking to tempt my unguarded mind away from all I held to be sacred and true. Defeated, the shaman grew angry, and said to me:

'Be warned! You are not ready to face the darkness. But

still the darkness will come to you. Your fate is locked to it. I have seen it is so.'

He spun around and his cloak swirled about him as he moved back into the gloom of the hut and shut the door behind him, his movement so lithe and quick that it seemed to my eyes as if he had simply vanished into the air.

'What were you thinking of – to enter into a pagan shrine in the company of a wizard?' Cadroc turned on me, his anger not yet abated. 'Have you no care for your eternal soul? Such a man may seek to enslave your mind or even cut open your body to perform vile auguries as a sacrifice to his devil-gods.'

'I could not help it,' I said. 'He pulled me inside and would not let me leave. You arrived just in time, Brother.'

'Well!' Cadroc's mood seemed to change immediately from that of righteous fury to one of real concern. 'This has been a frightening experience for you. It is over now. But what was it the wizard sought?'

'He… sought to learn about our mission,' I answered briefly. I dared not recount to him what had happened in full, for I feared it would not reflect well on me. I was appalled by my own feeble resistance to the wizard's power, but also profoundly shocked and disturbed by the realisation that he truly possessed such power.

'Of course,' Cadroc said. 'He fears my success, and the triumph of the Church.'

As we walked together to the village hall, I was further unnerved by the thought of the dark half-memory which had seemed to emerge in me during the ritual of healing. It had been of a thing utterly horrific in nature. I consoled myself with the notion that perhaps it was but a wild conjuration of my worst fears and imaginings or else only the distorted recollection of my hallucinations. But a dreadful doubt persisted, as I grew haunted by the shaman's words that the truth of myself, and of what I had seen, lay like a secret curse deep within me. Then remembered Brother Cadroc's firm contention that there were indeed demons who walked in the world with earthly feet.

Chapter Ten

We arrived at the hall, and as we entered its wide doors an old woman servant, who clearly expected us, bustled up and showed us to some shallow alcoves at the back, their floors covered in fresh straw, with folded blankets in the corners, where she said we might sleep that night. Then she led us back into the main hall, where the tables and benches stood, and said she would bring us food and drink. I asked only for bread, yet followed Cadroc's lead in taking some ale, relaxing my vow of abstention for reasons of good sense, as I supposed in this primitive outpost it might be safer to drink than the water.

We took our seats alongside Aelfric, who was already dining from a steaming bowl of pottage. As I began to eat, I noticed a stout and sturdy old man with a crop of luxuriant silver hair, a bushy beard and a very red face, who sat on the bench nearly opposite us. I nodded to him, but he did not respond, and seemed to regard us with an ill-tempered expression. He was drinking from a large jug of beer, and as he drank, I found him occasionally glancing across at us with a look that did not appear friendly.

My mind still felt distant and strange, but Brother Cadroc's mood seemed to become more relaxed as he said to me:

'And what did you make of that unholy spectacle in the wizard's den which you crept away to witness?'

'It was powerful... and moving,' I said, then added quickly, 'but of course distasteful to a Christian.'

'It was nothing!' he frowned. 'Nothing compared to what you will see as you go deeper into this world of heathen monstrosities. Here we are close to the borders of the tribe called the Spaldinga. It is said that compared to those savages, these Gyrwas are positively civilised. Yes, indeed. The deeper you journey into these Fenlands, the more irredeemably unchristian it all becomes and the farther from God you will find yourself.'

At that moment a young woman entered the hall, blonde-haired and strikingly pretty. She went across to converse with one of the men who sat nearby, and Cadroc's eyes followed her closely while a smile spread over his face.

'Ah, some of your Angle women are certainly very fine,' he said, his voice dropping to a whisper. 'How I should like to be closeted alone with *her*.' I stared at him in shock as he gave me a look that appeared almost lascivious. 'So that I might persuade her to accept the true Faith!' he explained as he saw my confusion. He looked about him suddenly and raised his voice. 'As a missionary one should always work hard to convert the women – especially young and pretty ones – for they are the surest way into the hearts of the men.'

'Yes! I know too well how you Christians work.' The red-faced old man spoke now in a slurred voice, having overheard these last words of Cadroc's.

'Good day, Edric,' Aelfric said to him, then gave me a wry grin as he raised his eyes to the heavens, and I guessed at once who this man was – the village drunkard.

The old man, Edric, took a huge gulp of beer, then poured himself some more as he went on:

'I am a Kentishman by birth, and Kent was the first of our kingdoms to fall to Christian corruption. And that was done by a trick with a woman.'

Aelfric sighed loudly, but Edric would not be silenced:

'Our old king, Ethelbert, may the gods curse his rotten soul, sold us out. Greedy old bastard. Kent was the richest of all the British lands, because we were the gateway and the main trading route into Europe. But trade wasn't enough for the Christian men of Europe. They wanted power and control over all our lives. So they bought our king with their gold, and inch by inch turned us into their vassal-state: everything run by Franks or Italians, officials and churchmen. And old Ethelbert, he just kept quiet and took the money. It was all arranged by the pope in Rome to stitch us up. Because you see, they wanted their Roman Empire back. But they couldn't get it by the sword, so instead they used stealth. They arranged for Ethelbert to marry a Frankish princess called Bertha. Of course she was a Christian, and she began to whine that she would only agree to wed a pagan king if she brought with her a bishop to be her "spiritual adviser". But this man's real mission was to become influential with the king and to learn his weaknesses – lots of them in Ethelbert's case – so that his Church masters could then exploit them. I heard that for some reason the Italians called these priests "Trojan horses". And the queen's bishop was only one move in a long-term bid to seize power. Look where it has led us. You scheming Christians have taken all our lands from us.'

He paused to take another great swallow of beer, and much affronted I said to him:

'It is not so. The Church is the instrument that will bind

nations together in a new and enlightened age…'

'My arse!' he growled at me. 'You only spout that horseshit, boy, to try and make people like me sound uncivilised. And don't look so offended. By the gods, your sort are always so eager to be *offended*.'

Now Cadroc rose to his feet, his expression at once transfigured with such wrath that he seemed about to lose control as his hand reached towards his sword. He stood for a moment, glaring at Edric, who shrank back at the sight of this fearful transformation.

'I will remind you,' Cadroc hissed, his face turning white, 'that it was your pagan forbears who first took these lands from my Christian people!' Then the astonishing moment was over, and Cadroc turned his back to stalk away and take a seat at the opposite end of the hall.

'You monks are all the same,' Edric began to mutter. 'All humility and mildness at first: how the Christ-god will protect us and win our battles for us if we worship him. But soon it all changes, and he turns into a monster who will condemn our souls to be tortured forever if we don't do exactly what you tell us. Christians say we no longer have need of our old seers and soothsayers, and this at least is true, since now we must only predict the worst possible outcome in all things to be proved right every time.' At this I rose indignantly to follow Cadroc; but Edric's hand shot out to firmly grasp my wrist. 'Wait!' he said, all his drunken belligerence rising, 'and I will tell you the truth about your Christian Church. In Kent I owned land which had been in my family for generations. But one day, in the beer hall on my lord's estate, I killed a man – a rich thegn's son – in self-defence. The man was drunk and out of control, and I had witnesses to swear oaths that my actions were justified. But his family was influential, and soon one of the king's judges – some doddering old thegn – came to hold an investigation, accompanied by his legal "assistant", a little weasel of a Frankish cleric. Throughout the hearing this man barely allowed the judge to speak without first whispering his instructions to him, while he studied the writings on his many pieces of parchment. They hardly listened to my defence or my witnesses, but soon returned a verdict that I had been found guilty of an unlawful killing. There was uproar among my supporters.

' "Since when has it been unlawful for a man to defend his own life?" I demanded.

'Now the Frank weasel stood to address the court directly.

' "It should be known to all," he said, "that the king has lately been engaged in revising this country's law code." Which meant of course that the king's Christian officials had been doing so in his name. The more corrupt the government the more plentiful the laws. "It is now the law that each case of this kind must be decided on close examination of the facts. For too long the excuse of a man's honour has been given to justify these drunken brawls. It is the view of the court that this fight, and a young man's death, might easily have been avoided, and now an example must be made."

' "But we were not told of these laws!" my own lord now objected.

' "That is not relevant to the case," the weasel answered him. "If you disagree with the judgement, lord, you are free to make an appeal to the king. But must I remind you that these are the king's own laws?"

'I doubt the king knew any more of them than we did. But now I was told I must pay the dead man's blood price to compensate his family, along with another fine to the king and his officers. And I was informed that under the new laws these fines had been greatly increased to serve as a deterrent. The sum demanded was simply ruinous. I knew that the value of my entire estate – all I owned – was unlikely to cover it. At best I would be reduced to slavery. And if I could not pay in full then the dead man's powerful kin would claim the right of a blood feud to seek vengeance and kill me. So I fled the court and took my horse and rode away into exile. But even as I ran I knew the truth of it. They were content to let me go, for they were not interested in me. Or in justice. What they wanted was my land. Kent is a small kingdom and land there is in short supply, but the Christians are always hungry to acquire it. What better way to take over a country than twist the law to condemn and outlaw native men of the old religion and steal their lands? So at last I ended up here, in this place of outcasts, and must live impoverished while some fat abbot or bishop holds everything my family ever owned. *Ah!* Fate goes where fate will.'

As he uttered this pagan proverb Edric's eyes grew blank and his head sank down, beer dribbling from the corner of his mouth as he relaxed his grip on me. I tore my arm free, then went to join Cadroc as I found myself becoming furious at these shocking accusations, for while I knew that individual churchmen were sometimes prone to human failings, I would not accept that the Church itself was corrupt. Surely it was the case that here was a guilty man so deeply angry and resentful that his words were only an embittered distortion of the truth?

Cadroc sat drawing deep breaths as it seemed he was still fighting to contain his mercurial anger. My own infuriation now seemed nearly as great as his, and I sat shaking while my mind felt exhausted and in a state of disorder after the tumultuous events of the day. Feelings of shame at my susceptibility to the shaman's trickery, combined with my outrage at Edric's drunken bile, were finally too much to endure. At last Cadroc looked up at me and said:

'You must forgive my outburst. I know it is my duty to bring the Word to such men and keep control in the face of their blind obstinacy. But it is a weakness in me that sometimes I lose patience with them. A fault I strive to address.'

'I understand your anger!' I said. 'You came here to protect and deliver these people, but they show no gratitude. And you cannot reason with a drunkard.'

'The truth is,' he went on, 'that my mission is for now my only concern. I have told you that my battle against this malevolent spirit is also a crusade against the blasphemies of paganism. The demon seems to me like a foul incarnation of the pagan soul itself: an outward manifestation of all its spiritual sickness and depravity. Do you know the heathens believe in something called a group soul? It is supposedly a merging in the afterworld of their spirits with those of their ancestors into a single mass consciousness.' His words reminded me of the strange sense of *oneness* I had experienced among the crowd at the shaman's healing. 'A fancy name for Hell!' Cadroc sniffed. 'But to succeed in my task will be to bring the true Faith of God to these people and save them from such grievous error. Yet my battle is also what will define *me*. Do you understand this? To gaze into the abyss, into the face of darkness itself, is the greatest test of a man – to pit himself against the power of Satan, always knowing that his soul might break. It is only there he will discover the truth of himself and learn the real measure of his faith.'

His eyes shone as he spoke, while I remembered my own failure of courage in the chamber of Lady Hild.

'Yes,' I said, at once inspired by his words. 'You have it exactly. It is for that reason I knew I must go with you.'

'But what now?' He raised an eyebrow. 'After what you have seen and experienced, is it your wish to continue?'

'Yes!' I answered firmly. 'I must go on. I see in your example much of the man I hope to become. And I certainly do not wish to be left behind in this ungodly place.'

'So be it!' he declared. 'I will let the decision be yours. Tomorrow we seek the trail again, and I fear it will not be long before it presents itself. Now go to bed. We leave at dawn.'

I bade him goodnight, then rose and left him. But after intoning my prayers, as I lay in my alcove I found that sleep did not come easily, and I drowsed there fitfully while my half-conscious mind drifted into a welter of strange imaginings. I conceived as a living reality Cadroc's allegory of a great pagan spirit made earthly and corporeal, grown savage and mad as the old faith slowly shrank away and died to cast it into the outer darkness, like the sinister masked figure of Winter in the spring festivals from my childhood or like the stories of the wild men consigned to their fastness in the remotest regions of the land.

Now I began to envisage this horror taking nightmare form, as there came to me a fleeting mental image that I stood and looked out across a night-darkened fen, and far away I saw something begin to stir and move deep beneath the earth, like a creature which was buried there alive, bursting upward as it tore itself out of the mire: an eldritch thing, mud-black, which fought and struggled to be darkly born into the waiting night. It appeared on the farthest edge of my senses, almost beyond the reach of my mind's sight. But I watched distantly as it clawed its way out from the blackest depths to emerge into the mortal world with murderous intent and claim for itself the ancient tributes of blood which men would now deny it.

My mind froze as it looked upon its own terrible creation.

But in a moment it was gone, the whole scene vanishing instantly as the balm of oblivion swept over me. Yet even as sleep gathered me into its dark embrace, and I knew my vision was the symbol of another reality, I also knew that what lurked deep in the swamp of my mind most surely had its grim and deathly counterpart in the living world beyond.

Chapter Eleven

I awoke with a start in the darkness, and looking up I saw one of the villagers standing outside my alcove, his figure illuminated by the dim glow of a burning rushlight.

'You must come now,' I heard him say. 'One of our men from the missing party has come back. I fear he is the last survivor of a terrible attack.'

At once Cadroc and Aelfric were on their feet, and I rose to join them as we followed the messenger out into the main hall. From there we were led outside into the blackness before dawn, to one of the dwelling huts, where we found a group of village men gathered about the one who had returned. Among these men I saw the shaman, but I carefully avoided meeting his eyes as we entered the house. Cadroc began at once to question the wretched man, who was filthy with mud, gasping and deathly pale, his hand trembling uncontrollably as he tried to drink from a mug of beer. In a while he composed himself enough to speak and give us his account.

'On the first day,' he began, 'we went deep into the marsh in search of fowl. Our hunting was poor, and when it grew late we thought to turn back, but then we say *no* – we are brave hunters who do not go in fear of tales of *thyrs* upon the fen. So we go to make camp for the night on wooded island of Weagar's Ridge, and plan to hunt again next day. There we started a fire and cooked duck, and drank from our flasks of ale till late. We slept, and in the morning when we woke we set out again on our hunt. But then a great fog came, and it was not safe for us to make the journey home. So we returned to our camp on the island and built our fire again, and again we went to sleep, but soon I woke up and must go from the camp to piss. It is now the attack comes. I heard great noise and much screaming. My companions cried out to the gods, but it is no help for them. I looked back, but...' here his face twisted with horror and shame '...there is a great fear upon me and I turned... and I ran. I heard that devil come after me, its footsteps pounding on the earth, and I rushed away far out into the marshes until I fell down exhausted to stay hidden. At last I rose up and fled, yet darkness came, and I lost my way and wandered far off, fearing always that the bogs would take me. Or the monster would find me. It is more by good fortune than intent that at last I find my way back home.'

'But did you *see* what attacked?' The shaman was first to speak. 'What did you see? What was this thing that came in darkness?'

'It did not come *in* darkness,' the man replied simply, his eyes bulging. 'It *was* the darkness! A giant thing made out of shadows. It was... the *night come alive!*'

At once Aelfric moved forward, wrapping his arms with great compassion about the shuddering man, and tightly embracing him.

'Try to calm yourself, Eadwine, you are safe now,' I heard him whisper, his face suddenly taut with a fierce grief and rage. 'There was nothing you could have done. I know what it is you suffer!'

Then Cadroc said to Aelfric:

'Do you know this place? The island of which he speaks?'

'It lies a league or so to the north. But it will be dangerous to travel over the marsh while it is still in darkness…'

'Damnation to the darkness!' Cadroc spat. 'We go now.'

'We must go with you!' One of the village men spoke up, a thickset fellow whose face was black with a seething fury. 'Our kin was in that company.'

'Prepare yourselves, and set out in full numbers at first light,' Cadroc told him. 'We must go on ahead, hard upon the demon's trail.'

'What of you?' Aelfric said to me. 'Have you still the stomach for this?'

'Yes,' I nodded, assuming a look of fortitude I did not feel at all. But my soul's path was fixed, and I knew that for good or ill I could not turn from it. I must face my great fear and put my trust in God – and in the powers of Brother Cadroc. From the corner of my eye I was aware of the shaman, as I felt his disconcerting stare upon me. Then he looked up, as if about to speak. But he remained silent. His malign presence made me feel relieved to be leaving, in spite of the terrors that might await us out on the fens.

We three departed from Meretun, and Aelfric led us out into the darkened marshes, brandishing a blazing torch as he picked our way forward with care, even as Cadroc urged him on with ever greater impatience, impelled by an urgency that seemed at once desperate and almost beyond his power to control.

'I go as fast as I dare!' Aelfric snapped back, his good-humour seeming at last to have deserted him. It had rained during the night, making our route ever more winding and difficult: the ground awash with stretches of open water, the mud-flats potentially deadly. I looked about me over the shadowy fen as the first light crept in, but the dawn came on so dull and overcast it seemed scarcely less gloomy than the night. And slowly it felt to me that the weird, rain-swept landscape began to blur gradually before my eyes into something like the threshold to an unearthly realm, where worlds of flesh and spirit might meet and join as one. Again the darkness of my imagination was overcoming me, as I wondered how anything which stalked alone in this desolate wasteland could be merely human; and there came upon me a powerful sense of oppression and nervousness as I thought back to that monstrous image which had seemed to surface in my mind during the shaman's ritual the day before. It began to feel as if I were being hunted and haunted by something deep within myself.

'Is it all well with you?' Aelfric asked me suddenly, perhaps noticing my look of uneasiness.

'It is strange,' I said, staring out across the bleak expanse of reeds and rushes that surrounded us. 'This land is so wide and empty, and we are so alone here, but I feel always as if it closes upon me to stifle me. It is a place to confound the senses.'

'The marsh has its moods,' he answered, 'and many will see in it the reflection of what is inside them.'

'You have the soul of a bard!' I told him, while I sought to master my growing anxiety.

As we moved onward the interminable mists swept over us, growing heavier as our route grew harder. Finally we approached the small island called Weagar's Ridge, which loomed forebodingly over the murk-shrouded marshes ahead, as I saw thick tendrils of fog that crept eerily through the tangled branches of its trees like a giant spider's web.

A sense of sheer unreality seemed to pervade the ominous

silence as we moved upward onto the solid earth, before negotiating a steep pathway through the heavy undergrowth. Now Cadroc took Aelfric's place in the lead, grasping the cross on his breast and drawing his sword as he told us:

'Stay back, both of you, and wait. I must go ahead.'

I stood for a time in silence with Aelfric, who appeared restless and eager to move, while all the pressures which had been accumulating in me now grew to become almost unbearable. As I surveyed the dreary terrain surrounding us, I began to imagine, as Aelfric had suggested, that all the brooding fears and shadows of my inner self were gathering to find solid form and substance somewhere beyond me.

'*Come!*' At last I heard Cadroc's sharp whisper from up ahead. Aelfric moved at once to join him, and I knew I must follow, although I had no wish to view the harrowing scene I surely knew would reveal itself to us.

As we moved to higher ground the fog thinned into a damp and clinging mist, drifting over the earth to cover like a gossamer pall the five corpses which lay scattered about the remains of a fire. The scene matched almost exactly that which I had witnessed at the outlaws' camp beyond my hermitage: the victims' bodies savagely mangled and their skulls crushed and broken in just the same way, with those fearful and inexplicable claw-like rakes and gouges. But it looked to me here that some of the faces of the slain were by comparison almost calm and tranquil in death, so swiftly must it have been visited upon them. With a sense of revulsion I turned away, to see the face of Aelfric as he stood beside me, his expression fixed in that same look of great agony and fury I had seen while he gave comfort to the distressed man at Meretun, and quite different from his largely dispassionate state at the last scene of slaughter. I reflected then that these were men who had been personally known to him.

'Our enemy has fled,' said Cadroc, 'but still we are close behind. So we go onward, and must follow the trail towards the northern settlements.'

As we left the dismal island and trekked back out onto the marshes, we each fell silent for a time and walked alone with our thoughts. But at last I turned to Aelfric and said:

'I believe there is something more for you in this mission than merely an instruction from the ealdorman.'

'It is so!' he answered. And after a long pause he went on: 'As a child I lived with my family on our farm on an island deep in the marsh to the north. When I was six there came a time of bad summer and great floods, and there was much famine in these lands. But ours was good land and spared the worst, and we grew enough to live. Then one day raiders found the secret path to our island – maybe bandits, perhaps hungry, desperate people from another farm or village. Yet I was small and to me they were like dark raging giants. Much afraid I ran to conceal myself inside a hidden cellar in our outhouse. My parents and kin were killed as they tried to defend our home, and I heard it all happen – terrible cursing and screaming – as I shivered underground, not knowing if I would be discovered there and murdered also. I could do nothing. *I could not help them*! Then I smelt smoke and I knew that our farmhouse was on fire and would be burnt to the ground. Terror made me helpless, and I froze and could not move, as I feared that the fire would spread and I would be burned alive. But these raiders took everything and left, and fire did not spread to the outhouse. At last I emerged, but all my family were dead and burned inside our home. Then I went off to live with my sister who was married into a clan which had farmland nearby. They were good people, but always afterwards I am troubled and restless. When I grew up I left, then wandered throughout the Fens until I came to know these lands well. Then at last I took service with Lord Ecbehrt. I was given this task at my own asking. Whatever it is we hunt – be it man or devil – I will see it die! So my duty will be done, and thus I hope the spirits of my kin will be in some way avenged. And their screams which haunt me still may also die.'

'Aelfric... I am sorry!' I said, reaching out to place my hand on his shoulder. He merely shrugged, and said no more as I began to reflect upon how the three of us were drawn together so strangely, each driven by some inner darkness to pursue the darkness outside. Of course I rejected the pagan concept of fate, but it almost seemed like our paths were weaved together in the pattern of some greater design.

My thoughts were suddenly interrupted, and we were halted in our tracks, as there rose at once about us a chilling sound: a long and terrific howl, a roar of primal rage which shattered the stillness and echoed out across the fen even as it broke and then fell silent. My heart began to pound as I searched my senses to locate the place of its source. Then I realised that it had come from behind us – it had come from back upon the island. I asked myself briefly if it might be the men arrived from Meretun to discover their murdered kin, but dismissed this conjecture, for it had been a single lonely cry and not the clamour of many. It had seemed like the sound of something savage and furious.

Now Cadroc turned and began to run back towards Weagar's Ridge, once more drawing his sword and calling out to us:

'Our quarry has eluded us. The demon is still here!'

Aelfric followed Cadroc and I went behind him, struggling to stay close and keep him in my sight as we entered back into the depths of the fog. As we reached the island and I climbed upward through its thick vegetation, I lost sight of them. I stumbled along a winding track, and Cadroc's dire warning returned to me as I realised with sudden alarm that I had strayed from the right path. But then with relief I saw a vague figure loom up in the murkiness ahead. Yet as I made to move towards it some deep instinct conveyed at once a warning to me, and then I simply froze: for as the figure drew closer to me and grew in form, I saw with profound dread that it was something of massive size, far bigger than either of my companions. I staggered backwards and then grew still, hoping the fog would conceal me as I felt my heart would fail. The ominous figure moved away and was lost in the gloom, while I remained fixed to my spot, not daring to stir or breathe, praying frantically in my heart for deliverance. It was as I began to hope the danger had passed that something fast and powerful sprang upon me with fearful force, gripping me from behind. A huge hand was clamped over my mouth, then I was lifted from my feet as if I were a child and thrown physically through the air, crashing down heavily onto my back. I gulped in a mouthful of air to cry out, but fell silent as I felt the tip of a sword press into my throat.

I grew numb as I looked up at the gigantic shape that stood over me, but even as I knew I was about to die, I was only aware that as I died I would at last look clearly into the face of the killer. It was the image I would take with me into death.

It was like a man, yet indeed one of extraordinary size and terrifying aspect, clad in tunic and trousers made from animal hide. The face appeared old and lined, and it creased into a savage growl as he bared his teeth at me. His hair and beard were long and grey, and he looked like a wild creature, a werewolf, a terrible merging of man and beast. As he stared at me he spoke in a whisper, yet his voice seemed to shudder in the air with pure menace.

'I know you!' he said from deep in his throat as his eyes gaped horribly at me. 'I have observed you in your place of refuge.' My mind filled instantly with the words of Aelfwin the carpenter, and what he claimed to have seen – something old and evil that was watching us. 'You seemed like only a mad pious creature obsessed by your dreary devotions, a harmless imbecile. But it may be you are more than you seem. Now you will tell me what I must know, and do not try to lie, for I will know it if you do. I will see into your heart and cut it out if I like not what I see. Tell me what you are doing here. What is your purpose?'

I looked up at him witlessly, not knowing how to answer as I lay in all senses upon a blade's edge. This savage was quite obviously insane, and a wrong word would surely be my last. But as I felt the press of sharp steel against my flesh, I knew in desperation that I must say something.

'Missionaries,' I stammered. 'We are only missionaries, who mean harm to none...'

'*Liar!*' I felt the tip of his sword push deeper, as I quailed with fear. 'I ask you for the last time what is your true purpose?'

'Monster!' I cried out, convinced now his claim to know truth from falsehood must be real. 'We have come to hunt a monster.'

'But you carry no weapon. So how will you fight?'

'With prayer!' I gasped.

'As I supposed!' he said. 'Tell me now what you have learned about this monster.'

'Nothing...' I said hopelessly. 'Truly... I know nothing...'

'He is mine!' His voice hissed suddenly with renewed fury. 'That devil is mine, for our souls are bound and our fates are one!' My mind was racing. What was he saying? That he was not the murderer? But he was clearly deranged, and who could tell what tormented fantasies might exist in his mind? 'You are hunting him with Christian magic,' he said. 'And now you will hunt him for me! I have seen his vile work – those murdered men whose bloody corpses lie nearby. He has returned and it is revenge he seeks. Upon all mankind. Upon *me!* He is a thing of vengeance and relentless hate!'

'Be calm, my friend.' I knew a faint sense of hope now as I heard Aelfric speak from somewhere nearby. 'Withdraw your sword. Please do not harm this innocent monk.'

The madman did not move, but stood, still scowling down at me, and kept his sword pointed to my neck. My eyes were fixed on it, and vaguely I saw it was a magnificent thing, the exquisitely forged weapon of a nobleman, and I wondered how it had come into the hands of such a creature as this. Then there were footsteps, and Cadroc emerged from out of the fog, his own sword pointed at the savage, who now seemed finally to relent, lifting his blade away from me as Cadroc strode fearlessly before him. But then the monk appeared to become astonished, and for a moment grew unsteady on his feet as the two men exchanged a long silent stare.

'It is you!' Cadroc said at last.

Aelfric now moved warily to my side and helped me to get up. I stumbled and nearly fell at first, for I could not feel my legs.

'It is the one they call "the Exile",' Aelfric whispered to me. 'He lives alone deep in the fen, and men avoid him in fear, for none know anything about him. We must keep our wits sharp. It might be we are in the company of the killer himself.'

I began to study the man. His manner was remarkably transformed, changed in an instant from murderous rage into composed silence. And I saw now that in spite of his wild appearance, his face when calm seemed stately and even handsome, and in no way truly monstrous. But the alteration in his mood had been so sudden and extreme – it was alarming. Perhaps he was really possessed by a demon. Who could know when he might turn back into a raging horror? It was as I considered these things that the truth of the matter came to me with sudden certainty.

'Do you understand this?' I whispered to Aelfric. 'This is the man Cadroc told us about – it is the wild stranger from his tale!'

I looked at him in wonder. But what was he doing here? And what did he know? Certainly his presence among us could be no mere coincidence. Suddenly he turned to me, looking huge and awesome as he stood half-shrouded in the heavy fog, and said:

'You must forgive me. I have been a long time alone, and my manner is rough. Men fear me and will not answer me willingly. It has been many years since I have known the companionship of others.'

Now Cadroc spoke, as he gazed with incredulity into the stranger's face:

'We must move on. The men from Meretun will arrive here soon, and when they find what awaits them their hearts will be filled with a vengeful fury. I cannot vouch for your safety among them. You will go with us!' His tone became at once demanding, and I feared for a moment it might rekindle the stranger's dreadful rage. But instead he seemed content to comply, and together we left the island to go back out into the marshes.

'I have followed your trail across these lands to find you,' the stranger said. 'When in these dark times I heard it said that a monk named Cadroc had come to the Fens, it was a sign I could not ignore.'

'This is the first time,' Cadroc said, 'that we were ever able to speak freely in a common tongue. I remember well those events in Elmet which brought us together so many years ago. But I have never heard your own story, and this you must now tell to me. It seems you know much I should hear.'

'I agree to this,' the stranger answered, 'since as you must suppose I have come here to seek your help. Your cause and mine have become once more the same.' He turned his head to look at Aelfric and me. 'You should know, all of you, that I was once a man and held my place in the world of men. It was long ago… long ago. Now I am what you see. No one before has ever heard my story. But now is the time to tell it, and this is the company to hear it.'

I could not imagine what kind of strange and terrible revelations his tale might hold, to have brought him to his present state. But so it was that he came to relate them to us.

Chapter Twelve

'My name is Cynewulf, son of Beornwulf, born to a noble clan in the kingdom of Mercia in the time of King Ceorl.

'The day of my birth was long afterwards remembered as one of ill omen. It happened in deepest winter, on a night dark and very cold, in the hall on my family estate at a place called Imma's ham – the home of the heirs of Imma. In those days, when Mercia was still a pagan land, the time of childbirth was given to the sacred rites and mysteries of women. When the pangs of labour began, the females in a village would gather at their place of worship to offer prayers to the goddesses Frigga and Freya. Then they would intone their ancient rituals to summon those great spirits who are the weavers of fate – Urd, Verdandi and Skuld – the Sisters of Wyrd. These three sisters would come to inspire a shamaness who would attend the birth, to act as a midwife, and then speak a prophecy of the child's future. In our kingdom at that time, the most famous and revered of these was a woman called Urta. It was Urta herself who came at my birth to perform this function, a tribute to the high standing of my family.

'Once the child was safely delivered, it was normal that the women would go chanting paeans from the place of confinement to give thanks and proclaim the powerful immanence of the Wyrd Sisters. Then they would burst into riotous celebrations, loudly daring any man to try and restrain them. They would dance and cavort, sing lewd songs, and go on to consume all the strong drink they could find. Like men in battle they would abandon restraint and later women would be found lying drunk and insensible all around the village. It was their time of freedom, and no man would seek to prevent it, for no man dared to forbid a woman who went under the spell of the Sisters.

'But I learned that when I was born these customary celebrations did not occur, for as my life began there blew up a sudden violent storm, and raging winds were followed by a blizzard that covered the land in ice and snow. That night many across the kingdom died, and among them was my mother. It was declared an accursed night. But still Urta fell into her trance, communing with the three Sisters to give her secret prophecy of my destiny to my grieving father. It was said that my father was never the same man after that night, and he never married again, nor even took a woman to his bed.

'As I grew older I was told of Urta's prophecy, and I once asked my father what she had foretold. But he only grew angry and would tell me nothing, forbidding me ever to speak of the matter again. I was never close to my father and was allowed little contact with him. He left me to be raised by servants, and they secretly supposed he resented me, blaming me for my mother's death. I once heard him shout at his steward, Herewald, that I was a changeling child of the dark elves. But I never really understood his aversion towards me and became bitter at his great unjustness.

'I grew, like my father, to be much taller and stronger than most men, and in my youth I was sent away to do military service with one of the king's ealdormen, Ceolwulf. It was made to seem like an honour, but even then I knew the harsh truth of it: I was to serve as a hostage to ensure my father's loyalty. How little they knew my father, if they believed that any threat against me would concern him. But in those days such rules were strictly enforced, for our king now was Penda, who had quickly come to assert his authority over our many feuding tribes and clans, and was turning Mercia for the first time into a strong and unified kingdom.

'I took well to the martial life, for my size and strength, along with my skill, made me a formidable warrior. I spent my young days riding through the kingdom, fighting to put down rebellion and lawlessness, and enforcing the king's authority. I rode in Penda's army to fight in his great war against the confederate lands of Northumbria, and I was twenty when he declared his first war against the kingdom of East Anglia. We marched behind him into Middle Anglia, the territory he sought to win from East Anglia's control, and our army gathered into three formations as we moved to face the enemy forces, while behind us there rose up the war cries and curses of our wizards. From the opposing ranks there came the chanting of monks, for it was known that Sigbert, East Anglia's king, a pious Christian, had gone soft in the head and retired into a monastery, leaving the rule of his land in the hands of his young kinsman. But his nobles dragged Sigbert, against his will, onto the battlefield in an effort to inspire his wavering troops. We saw him there, his standard surrounded not by warriors but by singing monks, and we all thought it looked very funny indeed.

'Upon the order we charged, shouting out our battle cries, and both shield walls met with a mighty crash, and almost at once the enemy formation started to break. In the chaos which ensued, I found myself face to face with a huge enemy warrior, who saw my own size and came forward to challenge me in single combat. I advanced and began to swing my sword in fast circular motions, a showy manoeuvre designed to demonstrate my skill and unnerve him. It did not work. He lunged at me, and as our blades met I felt at once his enormous strength. Then he was striking at me relentlessly as the air about us filled with the screams of men and the stink of blood. He was attacking so hard that I fell back before him as I smelt the reek of his stale sweat and looked into his wide, roaring mouth to see his rotting teeth as he bared them at me. Such was his sheer weight and power that we both sensed it was I who would weaken first. Desperately I saw that my best hope lay in my greater agility and speed, since I was a youth and he was a lumbering brute. But suddenly he stayed his attack, lowering his blade as if to rest his sword-arm. Exhausted, I sought a moment of respite to relax my own tortured muscles. Yet his move was a bluff, and he suddenly swung his sword at my face in a fast sideways strike. I raised my shield barely in time to block the blow, but in the same moment he struck out with his own shield, smiting me full in the face. The iron boss of his shield slammed into the nose-guard on my helmet, and I felt a sharp crunch of pain as the metal buckled and my nose began to bleed. I was stumbling backwards, my head ringing as my flesh crawled with fear, but I found my footing just as he came at me. Now I saw my chance, and I feigned another stumble as I waved my blade weakly in front of me, as if disoriented and still fighting to regain my balance. My opponent hurtled forward to claim his victory – my lure had worked. As he swung down his blade to beat mine aside, I pulled my sword back and leapt away, so his blow met no resistance as he lurched forward under his own momentum. I turned beside him, and with all my strength drove the point of my blade through his war-coat and into his ribs as he gave a bellow and the blood burst out through his chain-mail in a torrent. Then his life was mine for the taking.

'Already the enemy shield wall had collapsed, and they were in full flight as the battle turned into a rout. I joined the pursuit, but soon had to stop to pull off my helmet, for my nose had swollen painfully against the metal, and the stream of my own blood was suffocating me. I did not hear anything above all the confusion and clamour until it was too late, when suddenly there were footsteps running behind me. As I went to turn I was struck a heavy blow on the side of my head, and my sight began to fade as I fell dazed to the ground. I lay and felt the warm trickle of blood on my face and neck as I helplessly awaited the killing blow. But clearly my attacker had no time to inflict it, and I only began to sink deeper into unconsciousness.

'When I opened my eyes again I felt profound shock as I realised I could not move my body, but lay where I had fallen, entirely paralysed. I looked out over the mist-covered battlefield, strewn with the bodies of the slain, their faces fixed into lifeless contortions of agony and horror. The battle was long over, and the bodies lay stripped of their armour. A great terror filled my heart as it came to me that I had been abandoned, crippled and useless, and left for dead. I tried to call out to anyone who might be nearby, but my powers of speech were lost. So I lay, no more than a living brain housed within a corpse. Then I saw that the crows were beginning to come in great numbers to batten upon the fallen. And I felt sheer panic and terror as I knew that soon the carrion birds would come for me, to devour me while I was still alive.

'Now hordes of the creatures were flocking on the edge

of my sight, each one a little black horror as they flapped and hopped together in a vile scuffling mass until it seemed to me that these filthy things, which scuttled forward with beady, hungry eyes that seemed to exult in all my helplessness, began somehow to blur and merge within my sight into one obscene giant form that scrambled upon me in a single frightful movement, engulfing my whole body inside a great shroud of clawing, shuddering blackness.

'Wild fear overcame me even as I looked up to find that the darkness upon me was transformed and had become only a man who stood leaning over me to block out the sunlight.

' "Steady," he said to me. "It was a nasty blow. Can you stand up?"

'My head was splitting with pain, but the wound meant nothing. I felt only an incredible sense of relief to be restored to my waking self, so terrifying and real had the vision seemed. But now the living world itself appeared barely real to me as my senses grew vague, and I could find no power to speak or respond sensibly to my comrades, who supposed the blow had left me concussed and confused. I am sure it did, but over the following days it felt to me as if I were still helplessly trapped inside myself, lost and unable to communicate with the world outside, as the nightmare of paralysis I had suffered in my vision came to seem like a clear and fearful foreseeing of my present state. A cold fever plagued my body, while in the isolation of my mind creeping terrors began to grow: the memory of the flocking crows as they gathered into a single dark and predatory shape. I wondered what terrible events this image might portend. For I could not doubt that what I had experienced was something weird and ominous, yet hideously *real* – a grim and prophetic spirit which had entered into me, and which even now was not gone from me, but held me exiled and alone in a dark netherworld of inward foreboding and dread.

'At last my condition improved, and slowly I emerged to recover my normal senses. But since that time crows have been things of aversion and ill omen to me, and I will tell you that I still cannot look at one without shuddering.

'After our great victory there was peace in Mercia for some time, before King Penda began his warmongering again. Soon I returned home, since I had received a message informing me I was to be married. My betrothal had been arranged a few years before, to the daughter of an undistinguished thegn whose land bordered a part of our own. It was not a particularly advantageous match, and I wondered why my father had agreed to it. But I had seen the girl once – her name was Elswith – and she seemed pretty enough, so I supposed she would do. She was now sixteen, and her family were pressing for the marriage to take place.

'When I arrived back home, my father no longer seemed to me the intimidating figure of my childhood, for he had become visibly older in the years I had been away, and now I had grown even taller than he. I had not grown badly, I told myself, for a changeling of the elves. As a wedding gift he now presented me with something truly magnificent, designed to increase our family's prestige at the ealdorman's hall. It was a newly forged sword, beautifully wrought from the finest steel, the pommel studded with gleaming garnets. I named the sword Blood Drinker, and I have carried it with me to this day.

'The wedding ceremony took place on a cold, bright spring day in front of our hall. My bride and I stood to exchange our vows, surrounded by our families and retainers, who shook branches of the birch tree at us as the traditional symbols of fertility. I studied her face, beneath a lustrous crown of golden hair garlanded with spring flowers, and was not at all displeased by what I saw. But when she looked back at me she seemed to show no reaction at all, her eyes remaining blank and wholly dispassionate as she studied me. This offended me, for I was washed and scrubbed, finely dressed, and my hair was combed. I was tall and well made, even considered handsome, and she might easily have been married to some ugly troll three times her age. So in my youthful vanity I suppose I had expected her to be pleased with me.

'At the wedding feast we hardly spoke, and she answered all my questions with only a plain yes or no. She merely picked at the joints of meat served up on our trenchers, and I gained a sense of sulkiness and even anger from her. But I reminded myself that she was young and absent from her home for the first time, and no doubt unaccustomed to the company of strangers. So I decided I must be patient with her and treat her with kindness.

'But that night, when we were escorted to our bedchamber and left alone, the situation did not improve. Determined to do my duty – for that was how I thought of it – I threw off my clothes and lay on the bed beside her. But she only lay silently on her back, staring up at the ceiling with those perpetually angry eyes. I then tried to undress her, but while she did not resist she did nothing to help me, and indeed did not move at all. Her body was pleasing enough, with firm breasts and unblemished skin, but I was deterred by the pure coldness of her manner, and all the while she made no response to any of my fumbling efforts. What happened that night was awkward and embarrassing. It was like attempting to couple with a sack of dough.

'In the nights that followed nothing changed, and all my clumsy attempts were only met by this same icy lack of responsiveness. I had not known quite what to expect from her – I had spent my life among men and had little experience – but I definitely knew it should not be like this.

'Unable to endure her company for long, I began in the daytime to pass the hours in sparring with the men in my father's service, practising my swordsmanship and starting to accustom myself to the feel and balance of my new weapon. It was after a fierce bout, when my blood was roused, that I decided finally to go to Elswith and demand some explanation for her behaviour. I looked for her in our private room but did not find her there, and neither was she in the main hall, nor could I see her anywhere outside. I was informed she had last been seen walking out among the barns and outhouses, so I went to search for her there. It was while I wandered in that vicinity that I heard the faint sound of a muffled squealing. I traced it to a small storage hut, and quietly pushed open the door. My wife was inside, her back turned to me, and kneeling before her with her hands bound to a post and her mouth gagged was one of Elswith's maidservants. The girl was stripped, her gown flung onto the floor beside her; and my wife was inflicting a severe beating on her with a leather scourge. The servant's back was already bloody as she writhed and squirmed, but Elswith's fury was relentless, and each time she inflicted a blow she let out a short harsh cry, as if it were she who suffered the pain of it.

'I stood for a moment, entirely shocked, for whatever the maid's offence it surely could not warrant such a brutal punishment. I stepped behind Elswith, and as she raised the scourge to strike again I caught her wrist to restrain her. She turned on me, her teeth clenched and her lips curled instinctively into a snarl of anger. And in that moment I saw for the first time how my wife's eyes had come vividly to life.

But I saw something more. I saw the momentary rage and frustration of thwarted pleasure.

'I threw her from me as a feeling of pure revulsion began to rise, then I drew my knife and went to cut through the maid's bonds.

' "Dress yourself," I told her, "then go and get your wounds tended."

'As the maid stumbled away, I turned to face Elswith. Her eyes blazed at me.

' "What concern is it of yours," she spat, "how I chastise my servants?"

'I did not answer but reached out and grabbed her by her hair, then dragged her after me across the courtyard as she yelped and cursed and clawed at my hand. I took her to a cellar and flung her inside, telling the servants she was not to be released until I ordered it. Then I went to find my father.

'He was attending a meeting with a delegation of his tenants, but I was so angry I burst in on them and insisted I speak with him immediately. Furiously he ordered me to leave, but I bluntly refused and repeated my demand until at last he rose, glowering at me, and followed me into his private chamber.

' "I intend to renounce my bitch of a wife," I told him at once. "I want the marriage broken."

' "That is impossible," he growled at me. "The dowry lands are already passed over, and I presume the girl is no longer a virgin?"

' "The girl is a monster," I said. "There is something wrong with her."

' "Well, well," he laughed unpleasantly. "Then it seems I have a talent for matchmaking."

' "What is that supposed to mean?" I demanded in a rage.

And I began to understand that I had long been spoiling for a confrontation with my father. But he waved his remark aside, then asked me to tell him what was the matter. I explained to him what I had seen, but as he listened he only began to shake his head and assume a bewildered look.

' "What are you complaining about?" he said. "Your wife is entitled to discipline her own domestics."

' "In secret?" I looked back at him in astonishment. "Bound and gagged?"

' "Let me give you some fatherly advice," he sneered. "If your wife has offended you, then give her a beating. Although it sounds to me as if she might enjoy it. I have no time to discuss your childish quarrels. There are more important things for me to attend to."

'I understood that the tale I brought was of no great concern to my father. He had not been there in that dreadful moment to see the truth of my wife's vile nature revealed in her eyes. And it was difficult for me to speak to him of the travesty played out in our bed, for my father and I were in truth almost strangers. But it was his sheer refusal even to listen that enraged me most. I turned from him, clenching my fists as I sought to contain my anger.

' "I will not live with her as my wife," I said. "And I will no longer lay with her."

' "Then sleep apart," he answered. "What is that to me? But the marriage must stand."

'At once I turned back, glaring into his face, and what I saw there in that moment was unmistakably a look of cold satisfaction. And I knew then simply that *he had known.* Known all along the truth of my wife's nature. Now I saw clearly revealed the twisted reality of his hatred for me: to have schemed to find a wife he knew would be detestable to me, and I to her. But it was a thing that seemed to go beyond even a desire to destroy my happiness, or an act of revenge against me for my mother's death. It was still worse. For it appeared to suggest in him an insane wish to extinguish his own legitimate blood line.

' "You knew it all from the start," I said with disbelief. "You are mad." And I watched his body stiffen as he realised what I had finally understood. Then I roared at him: "I will have this mockery of a marriage broken!"

' "*You will do as I command!*" He burst suddenly into an explosion of rage, and all his self-control, every semblance of his sanity, was instantly gone. For the first time I saw the true madness of the man exposed. "You were always wicked!" he ranted. "A monster... an unnatural brat... a *thing* of evil omen. I should have strangled you at birth. *I was warned!*"

' "What?" I answered in sheer disbelief. "Ah! The prophecy of Urta, that you never thought fit to tell me. Now I have seen the truth of your insanity revealed, will you share that secret with me as well?"

' "Get out!*"* he screamed, and lurched away, covering his face with his hands as his body began to shake. "Go away and banish yourself. I cannot bear to look at you!"

'It was now at last I began to understand that all the hatred and bitterness locked inside him was not for me, but truly for himself. That for all these years I had been merely its object.

' "I am going!" I yelled back at him, turning and bursting through the door. "Why would I stay, with a raving lunatic for a father?"

'In the chamber outside the group of petitioners still stood, silent with shock at the terrible scene they had overheard. The servants came running to me in fear to ask what had happened, but I did not answer them, just shouted that I was leaving, but that I would return if only to take my revenge, for I had seen, even if I did not understand it, that my very presence was the cause of some dark torment and self-loathing in my father, and in my present rage I meant to come back to torture him further with it.

'But first I had a mission to undertake. For I was now determined I must learn the truth of this whole dreadful matter. And I saw only one way in which to do it. I must seek out the seeress Urta.'

Chapter Thirteen

'It might be difficult to trace the whereabouts of Urta –
if indeed she were still alive – but I knew I must make the
attempt. I rode first to our local temple to make enquiries of
the priests there. They were uncertain, until the elderly chief
priest came to inform me that he had been told she had retired
in old age to the village of her birth, a place somewhere on the
western tip of the Fens. If I rode there, I might seek further
information from local sources.

'The weather turned bad, and for the next two days I
journeyed in perpetual rain until I came to the edge of the
great marshes, where the ground grew boggy. As I rode there
I started to feel feverish and my head began to ache. I still
had a weakness there from my injury in battle, and soon I
found myself overcome with feelings of intense dizziness and
sickness, and was unable to ride on. Nearby I found a lonely
cottage, and leading my horse I stumbled up to it to seek help.

'The cottage was only a bare and abandoned shell, and
looked as if it had stood uninhabited for some time. But the
remains of the hearth were still intact, so I tore away lumps

of wood and straw from the driest parts of the inner structure and roof, and built a fire there. I had brought with me some supplies of food and water, and for several days I remained inside, only stumbling out occasionally to attend to my horse, otherwise shaking and sweating at the hearth-side as my condition gradually improved, until finally I felt sufficiently recovered to continue at a slow pace on my journey.

'Information gained from settlements and temples along the way now gave me strong hopes that Urta was indeed still living, and on a damp cloudy morning I rode at last into the village where she was said to dwell. It lay upon the very edge of the Fens, where a narrow strip of firm ground led like a pathway onto what was otherwise an island entirely encircled by the marshes. I led my horse into the main village, and soon the head-man, along with several others, came respectfully to meet me and ask my business. He pointed to an outlying hamlet in the distance, and told me that Urta's cottage lay there, then sent a slave to escort me along a muddy track towards it.

'The cottage itself was a run-down structure, its timber nearly hidden beneath a sagging, rain-soaked roof of reeds and straw that sank almost to the ground. It stood at the farthest end of the settlement, close to where the marshes began. As I approached it a woman emerged, middle-aged with dark hair and a severe expression – surely too young to be Urta herself.

' "What is it you want?" she said to me abruptly.

' "I must speak to the shamaness," I said. "On a matter of importance."

' "Mother Urta rarely agrees to see anyone any more."

' "I am Lord Cynewulf," I told her. I had expected my rank alone to gain me entry, and I was tired, and angry to be questioned by a servant in this way.

' "You do not understand," she insisted firmly. "I see you

are a man of position, but such things do not matter to our Mother Urta. Her mind is distant, and these days she lives much in the Otherworld, far from all earthly concerns. A man's rank is of no consequence to her."

' "Inform her that Cynewulf of the house of Imma waits upon her," I said, "or I will go in and announce myself."

'She paled slightly as she looked up at me and saw my anger, then motioned to me to wait, and turned to go back inside the cottage. Soon she returned with a disconcerted expression to announce that Urta would receive me. I bent down to squeeze beneath the low doorway, then prepared myself to show due deference to this old harridan, whose name had always seemed to haunt my very existence.

'She sat deep within, upon a rug on the floor, ensconced in the gloom beside a faintly glowing hearth, while candles burnt eerily all around her. It felt truly like I was stepping into the Otherworld. Gradually my eyes accustomed themselves to the dimness, and I saw that everywhere around me was a chaos of magical paraphernalia: strangely shaped plant roots, animal bones, a human skull which stood upright upon a pole, dead shrivelled snakes, the wings and limbs of birds, odd figurines carved from stone, crystals with runic symbols scratched upon them, and much more. All were scattered about the room in no discernible pattern or order. Urta sat in the midst of all this confusion, looking down at the floor while she played with a collection of rune sticks, tossing and then studying them where they fell, craning down her neck to focus her bleary eyes on their upturned symbols, then gathering them up to throw them again as she hummed softly to herself. She seemed to be oblivious to my presence.

'She was ancient: shrunken and wizened, her cheeks hollow and her white hair hung in lank strands, with patches of flaking scalp visible beneath it. Her green robe, far too voluminous for her withered body, was covered with dirt and stains. She looked like an animated corpse.

' "Greetings Mother," I said, now wholly intimidated as she looked up at me. She was truly a dreadful sight, her eyes sunken into their sockets, her mouth shrivelled and toothless as she leered at me. "I have come to ask your help. I need you to remember an event that happened more than twenty years ago. But I am sure you will recall it. It took place at my home, in Imma's ham, and it was on the night of a great blizzard – the night of my birth. My mother Aelswyn died that night. You were there, and gave the birth prophecy to my father Beornwulf. I must know what happened on that night. Please will you tell me what you can remember of it?"

' "I cannot do so!" She blinked at me, and her head began to jerk in a birdlike way as her shrill voice rose, and her face assumed a look of wariness. She regarded me as if I were only a distraction from other more real concerns. "I cannot repeat any prophecy I may once have given. The words I speak are sacred and secret, and it would anger the spirits were I to reveal them."

' "But the prophecy was given for me," I implored. "I must explain. Over the years the memory of what happened that night has driven my father to madness. He will not speak of it, but I must know what has done this to him. You, Mother Urta, are my only hope."

' "It cannot be done... cannot be done. It is more than my powers are worth!" She squinted and frowned at me. Then she said: "Do you know that I am much honoured by the king?" Her withered body seemed to puff itself up with pride. "Oh yes, King Ceorl holds me in high regard."

'I looked at her in dismay. King Ceorl had been dead for ten years. This woman had lost her wits. Old age and the spirits had stolen them away. I reflected hopelessly that my journey had been a wasted one.

'But suddenly there came upon her ravaged features a look that was deep and powerfully intense, as her eyes glared defiantly into mine. And then I felt that something strange was happening. I found myself fixed to the spot, while all her anger and indignation seemed to melt away. It felt in that moment we became locked together in a kind of deep and silent struggle. Then her mouth fell open, and her eyelids began to flutter, then drooped shut. She seemed to fall instantly asleep, her head sinking down as her breaths grew deep and stertorous. As I watched her I became oddly affected by this, as my own breath caught in my throat, and the deathly stillness and the acrid smell of burning wood which filled the air in the hut felt at once suffocating and overpowering – as it seemed now my senses were elevated to a level of incredible sharpness. I knew then a distant stirring of fear and alarm, as I felt myself alone, confused and helpless. My flesh grew cold and I began to tremble, and for the first time, I started to doubt my own purpose in coming here and entering this horrible place to learn forbidden secrets which perhaps it were better to remain unknown.

'Suddenly the coldness about me became so intense it was like an icy wind which chilled my skin and froze my blood. A profound dread had come upon me – the creeping sense of some other time and place – robbing me of the power of motion: a feeling that I had entered into some dark unearthly realm or sphere, which instilled in me a rush of shock and fright beyond anything my mind was able to resist or oppose, while the frail tiny figure of the witch now seemed to my eyes to have become one of awesome and terrifying supernatural power.

'Now I heard a voice begin to drone in the distance, and I supposed it must come from Urta, although its tone seemed light and girlish, like a child speaking a nursery rhyme, but in a way that was mocking and sly. But my heart was stricken with fear, and I found I could not stir but only listen as the voice began to recite a verse that was distantly familiar to me: some lines from one of the grim old poems I had sometimes heard spoken by the *scops* at the ealdorman's hall:

' "There goes a man who walks alone, along a dismal track,
His path is wild, his way is lost, the moon is at his back,
He hurries on and does not turn, upon the dreary fell,
For stalking close behind him comes an enemy from Hell.
A blood-cursed thing that creeps outside the light enjoyed by men,
The moor and marsh its stronghold, its lair the haunted fen."

'The voice laughed softly, a faint ripple in the darkness. Then it spoke again, its tone growing cold and brittle, almost inhuman, as if it rang out from the halls of the dead.

' "I saw a man whose fate followed him like a demon in the dark… a night-roaming thing… it moved implacably behind him… it rose and loomed over him… and in the moonlight its twisted shadow consumed him… until I no longer saw the man. *He was gone!* And where he had walked… only the shadow remained… only the monstrous shadow…" The voice gave a sudden groan, then called out in a low harsh whisper: "Do you know what is a dark *fetch*? It is our soul's shadow, a spectral double, a spirit twin. It is the manifestation of our darkest self. In a damaged psyche it may be split away and divided from the whole – the lost fragment of a soul. Frozen in time, it will wander alone and apart, like a disowned and

158

abandoned child, and its anger and resentment will grow, filling it with all the rage of the outcast. Beware it, for it is yourself, and your hatred will make it *deadly!* "

'There was a quick intake of breath, another gurgle of laughter, and my body was soaked with sweat as dread coursed with unbearable intensity through every frozen nerve. But in a moment my fit of terror was lifting, as the blank eyes of Urta suddenly opened and looked up into mine. Now fully awake she appeared to forget my presence entirely as she went back to playing with her rune sticks and muttering nonsense to herself. At once I felt utterly foolish, then grew furious to think I had allowed a dribbling old madwoman to terrify me so, and render me powerless.

'As I left her and came back out into the daylight, I knew a sense of relief as my worldly mind reasserted itself, and it seemed to me then that I stepped out from under a cloud which had darkened my whole existence. I did not doubt many believed Urta's insane babbling to be a sign of her prophetic gifts, but I would not permit myself to be so easily deceived. Then my heart became filled with pure anger as I thought of my father, and how he had allowed his mind to be turned, and his life – and mine too – to be blighted by the demented ramblings of that old charlatan. I resolved then to return home at once, confront him again and tell him bluntly he was a weak-minded fool.

'When at last I came back to Imma's ham, I felt immediately that something there was wrong. Everywhere was still and hushed, and the place seemed almost deserted, with no one going about their usual business. The few I did see turned their faces from me and hurried away. When I came to my father's hall, his steward Herewald appeared at the door, his face grim and pale, and he motioned urgently for me to join him inside.

' "Lord," he said, his state one of extreme distress. "Your

father is dead. Horribly murdered."

'I looked at him in disbelief for a time until I found the power to say:

' "How?"

'He trembled, then took a deep breath as he prepared to tell the story.

' "After the day of your great quarrel, the day that you rode away, Lord Beornwulf fell into a black mood. He shut himself in his chamber and would see no one. Then, on the second day, he emerged to announce that he would go to stay at the old hunting lodge, at the far end of the estate, on the edge of the forest. This was most odd, since the lodge is in great disrepair, and in the past your father had never seemed to like it there, indeed always neglected it. But none of us cared to question him in the mood he was in, so preparations were made and he set out with only a small party of attendants and servants.

' " The day after they arrived, in the morning, your father took a spear and a bow, and said he would spend the day hunting in the forest. His men offered to go with him, but he refused and said he preferred to go alone. He came back before sunset complaining he had found no game. That night he called to him his hearth-man Offa, and they spoke privately. The next day Offa set out alone towards the forest on some unknown mission. No one knows where he was headed, and he has not been seen since.

' "In the night the household was roused from sleep by a terrible crashing and commotion from your father's chamber. They burst through the door to find…" Here he paused, and for a moment could not go on. "They found the rotting shutters of the window smashed through. A torch burned in the sconce and they saw at once that someone had broken in from the outside. Your father lay in the bed, soaked in blood, his body stabbed and mutilated all over. His people gathered about him, and as they looked at him in horror they saw that in his mangled flesh a trace of life yet remained.

' " 'Lord, who has done this?' they urged him. His eyes opened, and with his final breath..." Herewald reached out to clutch my arm "...he cried out: 'My son! *My son!*' "

'I looked at Herewald in shock and desolation. Could it be so? That my father with his dying breath would condemn me as his own murderer? Could such hatred exist in a man's heart? Tears sprang into Herewald's eyes as he went on.

' "I have known you from a child and I could never believe this. Your father's mind was in shock and he did not know what he said. But can you account for where you were on the fourth night after you left? Have you any witnesses who can swear to it?" I shook my head hopelessly. Upon the night in question I had lain alone, sick and sweating, inside the deserted cottage. "But there were many witnesses," he said, "to the violence of your parting quarrel and your own threats of vengeance. Word of this has been sent to the ealdorman, and soon officers of the king's justice will arrive to investigate. My poor boy. The case against you is damning."

' " I must flee!" the words rose as a sob into my throat. "He has taken everything from me with his last breath. My home... my name... my life. I will be condemned as a patricide. Hunted and hated... detestable to men. I will be a *nithing*... a criminal and an outcast forever."

' "You must go," he said, "before the king's men come. May the gods help and protect you. But now you should go into the forest. There are many places to hide there, but also it may be that you will discover some clue to Offa's mission, or even find Offa himself. His story might shed some light upon this matter. It is a small hope, but your only one."

'We gave each other a tearful farewell, for since my childhood he had been the nearest thing I had known to a father. Then I rode away. I was never to see my home again.

'I made my way into the forest. Following the path which led from the hunting lodge, I found after the recent rains there were still tracks visible in the muddy ground. I followed these along twisting pathways through the thickening woodland, my mind filled with a despair that increased as my initial shock abated, growing darker with every step to match the deepening gloom of the forest. I found now the echo of Urta's words began to haunt me, and that I could no longer simply dismiss them. She had spoken of my dark *fetch* – my disembodied spirit. I was familiar with the belief that at times our souls might wander free from our bodies, while we sleep or during times of illness when we are closest to the realms of death. It was said that violent and disturbed emotions might even give them powers in the physical world, and, freed from the restraints of its earthly existence, an angry *fetch* could become a turbulent and dangerous thing. Urta had also spoken of a disowned child, and of its rage and resentment. Then at last I began to wonder whether my father's accusation might be true, and if some lost and vengeful part of my own being could have risen to commit this dreadful crime?

'I passed gradually into the deepest regions of the woods, following with increasing difficulty the faint tracks which would vanish and then suddenly reappear in places so overgrown and wild that they became almost impenetrable. Until at last I was distracted from the misery of my thoughts as I came suddenly upon a woodman's cottage, a crumbling hovel that nestled under a high bank, surrounded by trees and almost hidden from view. It stood there, incredibly remote, many miles from any other human habitation. I approached it, calling out to let any within know of my presence, but no answer came. The place looked deserted. So I went to the door and entered.

'Inside it was sheer chaos. Three corpses lay on the floor. One of them was Offa. A broken stool lay beside him, the wood stained dark-red with his blood, for his skull had been brutally smashed in. The other bodies I supposed to be those of the woodman and his wife, both old, and going to examine them I saw that both had been killed by a sword – presumably Offa's sword. Yet now there was no sign of that sword in the room. Which meant a fourth person had been present. But what part had they played, and where were they now? Why had Offa come here to kill these people? I saw no reason behind any of it.

'But now my blood froze as I sensed instantly the presence of another inside the room. And turning back towards the door I saw him there, at the threshold, a creature that was barely like a man at all. He was taller and bigger even than me, his hideous face slack and dribbling, his savage gaze fixed on me, simply fiendish in its look of sheer malevolence. He was dressed in rags, and beneath them his body appeared squalid with dirt and grossly misshapen: a disgusting thing half finished by nature, if indeed he were a natural being at all. Because, as I stared rigidly into his face, I slowly realised something terrible. You will note that my eyes are of a distinctive hue – of deepest and darkest blue, a trait inherited from my father. I now saw with disbelief that what looked like my own eyes stared back at me from out of the corrupt frame of this monstrosity, and then I began to realise that his very form and features were like a vile and distorted mockery of my own. I could not deny the horrible truth that this creature bore unmistakably a grossly deformed resemblance to *me.*

'In that moment I feared Urta's words had been true, and this was indeed a manifestation of my dark *fetch*. I let out a cry as I tottered backwards in sheer terror. But then the horror seemed to burst into a rage, and he sprang towards me as I saw that in his huge hand he held Offa's sword. I drew out my own sword, determined to drive away this grisly apparition, to see it dissipate into the air. As our blades clashed together I felt that his strength was simply immense. Yet he had no skill. I drew back my sword and struck out wildly, cutting a gash into his arm. He dropped the sword as red blood started to gush from his wound, and he unleashed at me a terrifying screech of pain and fury. Then he turned and was gone, bounding away swiftly to be lost within the depths of the forest.'

Chapter Fourteen

'I staggered out of the cottage, and my strength deserted me as I toppled down onto the grass and buried my face in my hands. My head was spinning as my brain attempted to untangle and make sense out of what I had just witnessed. There had been *blood*. I looked up to see the trail of red spots that led away from the cottage, staining the ground along the way where the creature had fled. So I knew now that he had been no spirit – no *fetch* – but something of living flesh and blood.

'I sat for what seemed to be hours, as gradually my mind attempted to impose order on all its turmoil. But constantly the words of Urta returned to me, rushing through my thoughts, until at last I began to find reason in what before had seemed like only madness. She had spoken in her trance of one followed by a shadow-thing – a *twin soul*. She had been present at my birth, and somewhere inside all the confusion of her aged and addled brain *she had remembered*. Indeed she had remembered. For how could she ever forget the birth of a monster? The birth of my own twin.

'Now at last I understood my father's terrible secret, which had unbalanced his mind and come finally to devastate my own life. Urta's prophecy had pronounced him cursed by the gods, and he had seen that his line was blighted. It is said that in ancient times the blood of giants and monsters sometimes became mingled with the blood of men. Perhaps this was not the first time it had happened: maybe there had been hushed warnings, old and fearful whispers in our family of a taint in our blood. Of the birth of monstrous children. A mark of vile disgrace, a cause of shame and ignominy, a black stigma upon our name should it ever come to be known. But it seemed that in spite of Urta's warnings, my father had not been able to kill his own child. So it was hidden away, never to be mentioned, sent deep into the forest into the custody of childless servants who would keep it there beyond the sight and knowledge of anyone. Yet forever after, stricken with horror, tormented by the memory of Urta's words and obsessed by the knowledge of his curse, my father in his growing madness was never able to look at me without seeing *him.*

'But then came our great confrontation over the matter of my wife, and when he saw in my eyes the accusation of what he was – of the monster *he* had become – my father brooded. And he went into the forest to look upon the secret thing he had spawned, now fully grown, and decided finally that it must die. But still he would not do it himself. So he sent Offa – his oldest companion and perhaps his confidant and accomplice in this matter from the start – to carry out the deed. I could not know if he had also ordered the deaths of the old couple, as witnesses to his shame, but it seemed to me most likely they had died simply attempting to protect the child they had raised as their own. But my father had misjudged his monstrous progeny, made docile in the presence of his keepers, and had supposed him to be only a harmless idiot, not recognising the true rage and savagery concealed in his nature. Yet these passions were inflamed when he saw those who had been his parents, and his life's only companions, murdered before his eyes. And his mind had understood that the man who had earlier come to look at him, the powerful lord who doubtless regarded him with an unconcealed detestation, had sent the assassin to kill them. So the wretch – I could not bring myself to call him my brother – had crept out into the world of men, and there taken his revenge. My father's murderer was indeed his own son.

'I sat and turned these ideas over in my mind, but quickly became convinced of their truth – I could find no other explanation to fit the existing facts. So I sank down, curling up my body on the ground, wishing that I might sleep, to awaken later and find I had only dreamed these events which had torn my world apart in the course of a single dreadful day. But I could not rest, and knew that at any time the king's men might come to search for me in the forest. I must move, and distance myself, for how could I expect anyone to believe the wild story I had to tell? I must accept that my old life was lost to me, and my guilt would seem to be confirmed to others by my very act of running. But then I saw there remained one last chance for me to prove my innocence and regain my name – to pursue the real murderer. I must hunt down the miscreant whose polluted blood ran within my own veins. This idea at once impressed itself upon me with a startling clarity. My father's cruel actions had unleashed a brute upon the world. The wretched circumstances of his life were indeed tragic, and I might have felt a sympathy for him, but his body was too grossly deformed, his mind too damaged, for me to allow myself any such emotion. I had seen too clearly in those few moments the hateful and violent nature which burned in his wicked soul. It bore a spite to embrace all mankind. He had blasted my life into ruins and would so afflict the lives of others if left to roam free. It would indeed be an act of mercy to all – himself included – to destroy him like a mad dog. And then, any who looked upon his hideous corpse would surely accept my assertion that here was my father's true murderer? Yet I saw now how this matter went even beyond establishing my innocence. It went deeper still. For I also knew this task was mine alone, allotted to me by the Fates themselves. It was a matter of duty, honour and blood, and now the only legacy my father had bequeathed to me.

'I felt convinced the wretch would not return again to the cottage, for he now knew this lair to be discovered, and I sensed in him a devilish cunning. And so, driven from his hiding place, it surely would not be difficult to run him down, for how could such a creature go undetected for long in the world of men? But I must also go with caution and remember that from this time onward I would be an outlaw and a fugitive.

'At last I stood up and began to move, following along the way where my twin had fled. After several hours the woods grew thinner and I was able to mount my horse and ride, but now the night began to fall, and I knew it would be impossible to continue my search in the dark. It was as I reached the edge of the woods and entered onto an open stretch of land that I heard an outcry of distant voices raised in desperation and alarm. As I rode towards them I saw in the fading light ahead a small settlement, a farm which lay in near darkness save for several men who moved within its confines and carried lighted torches. It was as I approached them that a dog ran at me, barking furiously, then I heard a woman's voice shriek out above the rest.

' "A joint of bacon! *A joint of bacon!*"

'I knew a sinking feeling in the pit of my stomach as I rode up to the men and called out to them, and they drew forward, armed with spears, mattocks and knives as they peered at me through the dimness, their breaths gasping and their dull eyes glinting with shock and horror in the yellow glow of the flames.

' "What has happened here?" I said, although truly I feared the matter needed no explanation. They stood in silence, staring up at me nervously, their faces taut with rage and grief until finally one stepped forward and said:

' "An attack, lord. It came with the dusk. It burst into our father's cottage as he sat with our mother to eat…"

' "It?" I said.

' "Yes," he answered, his voice close to breaking. "Our mother says… it was not a man but a giant. A monster. A *thing* of evil omen…"

'I looked back at him, struck mute as I saw that his words were those my own father, in his mad fit of rage, had thrown at *me*.

' "…and our father rose to stand before our mother and protect her, but the monster carried a thick stave of oak – we think taken from our barn – and fell with devil's fury on him, and beat in his head before it snatched up their meal and was gone. We heard our mother's screams and came, but too late… we saw only a great shadow fleeing in the distance. We feared to pursue it into the darkness."

' "Which way did it run?"

'He pointed with a trembling finger out into the forest, as the distraught voice of the woman rose up again from somewhere behind him.

' "He is dead… for a joint of boiled bacon!"

' "I give you my oath," I said to those men, as wrath gathered in my heart, "that I will hunt down this monster and destroy him. Your blood-feud is also mine, and I swear to you I will not stop until all our wrongs have been avenged."

'I turned my horse and rode away into the night.

'So began the mission which would consume my whole existence. It became my life's only object, my singular fixation. The path was long and hard. The seasons came and went as I journeyed through sun and rain and snow, across fen and moor and forest, through different lands, finding and losing then finding again the trail of the one I sought. I followed every dark whisper and rumour, hearing fearful, half-known tales repeated of a lone raider, huge and terrible, who preyed upon the lonely homesteads and farms, coming silently with the night to gain his sustenance: to attack, steal and murder with an inhuman ferocity and strength. But always he eluded me and remained ahead of me, leaving in his wake only a trail of atrocities to taunt me. I had been wrong to suppose it would be easy to find him. I had failed to imagine the reality of it. At night, when I travelled over high ground, I would look far out at the distant flickering of camp fires in the remote scattered villages, like tiny pale stars within the great black firmament of the wilderness which encompassed them. Those vast hostile wastelands were his domain, from which he would rise then vanish like a phantom moving between the mortal world and the realm of the dead. And my task grew slowly to seem daunting and hopeless. But forever I must move on, never daring to stay in any place for long, shunning the company of other men for fear that my own dark history should overtake me.

'My horse sickened and died, and so I continued on foot, living the best I could, stealing when I must. My appearance grew so wild and ragged that men often feared me and fled at my approach, until it seemed to me that I had come to appear barely different to others, from the one I pursued.

His shadow had indeed consumed me utterly. Now I had to gain my information by means of menace and threat – by the fear I inspired. And gradually I lost all thoughts of my old existence and of proving my innocence – by now my title and estates would have passed to some other, and I... I no longer cared about them. My mind was fixed only upon my enemy, and life itself had come to mean nothing to me beyond the consummation of my final revenge.

'Then at last the trail grew cold as my adversary seemed to vanish without trace, and for many seasons I wandered without hearing any word of him. But now my mission had become my life and to give it up was unthinkable to me. Finally I journeyed back to the northernmost reaches of my own land, where a long while earlier – I could no longer keep track of time – I had last heard fearful reports of him. From there I went up to where the woodlands of northern Mercia darkened into the great forest of the Celtic land of Elmet.

'One night, as I slept deep in the forest, somewhere close to the Mercian border, I was woken by the sound of a distant voice rising up out of the darkness. Growing curious, I drew my sword and moved cautiously among the trees into the night, guided onward only by the voice ahead. Then I spied the light of a burning torch, and the words grew clearer, as I recognised them as being spoken in my native Anglish. It was the voice of a man which rose and fell as he recited an invocation to a god.

> ' "I face the east and pray for favour,
> I call to the coming dawn.
> Hear us, great protector.
> Deliver us from what blights the land,
> From the terror that walks in the night.
> Look with favour on our offering of blood."

'I stepped up to a small forest glade, and raised my sword as I saw a group of four men standing inside it. As I went, fallen twigs cracked under my feet, and these men turned to face me, their eyes wide with fright. Before I could move or speak, all four combined their voices into a single cry of panic and terror, and then they were away, the torch bearer flinging his brand onto the ground as they scattered beyond my sight. As I stared after them, I began to consider the words of the chant I had heard uttered. From what dark power had they prayed for deliverance? And what was their offering of blood?

'I moved to where the discarded torch lay still burning, snatching it up, then began to search the ground around me; until I came upon a human form there, lying prostrate, silent and motionless, in an effort to remain unseen. As I approached it, it began to wriggle forward, struggling in its efforts to rise, as I observed that its hands were bound behind its back, and that a length of rope was hung about its neck, beneath a wild tangle of hair. At first I took it for a child, as its frame looked small and slight, but as I drew near it turned its head to look up at me with wild and frantic eyes as it bared its teeth in a snarl; and I saw that it was a young woman. Her dark hair probably marked her as a Celt, and she was clad in the rough single garment of a slave. Plainly her life was to have been given as an offering, and I felt a dull sense of shock, for I had not supposed that even crude forest dwellers, such as those men had been, were so primitive that they still practised human sacrifice.

' "Do not be afraid,' I called out to her. "I will not hurt you."

'I took her arm and raised her up, but she struggled and cried out, and I tightened my grip as I brought up my sword to cut through her bonds. Then I turned her about to face me. Ragged as she was, pale and trembling from her fearful ordeal, I was struck by her comeliness, but more by her appearance of fierceness and courage as she stared back at me, allowing no sign of fear to show. I released her, and stepped away to reassure her that I meant no harm. As I stood, hardly knowing what to say, she spoke out in the babble of her own tongue; then, seeing I did not understand her, she began to talk in muddled Anglish, presumably learned from her time as a captive.

' "Those man say I be bad slave. More trouble than worth. You no want to keep me. Angle man come raid, catch me out in forest, take me from free and keep me bound, shut me in place under ground, or else say I run. Or I steal knife to cut throat in night. They say true. I be glad, kill them all. Catia *is* bad slave. You take Catia for slave, one day she kill *you*."

'I was astonished by her words, or rather how she spoke them with such defiance in spite of her desperate circumstances. It was born of a pride which had endured undaunted even in the face of such terrible adversities. Her spirit seemed to dwarf the bravery of every warrior I had ever known.

' "Catia," I said. "I am Cynewulf, and I give you my promise that I would not try to bind such a soul as yours." She looked at me strangely, and the fire in her eyes was then diminished by a look of confusion. Probably she had expected nothing but harshness from any man of the Anglecynn. So I said to her slowly: "You have your freedom, to return to your own people." Still she stared back, and seemed unable to comprehend. "You are free," I said, for it appeared I could not convince her.

' "Not free," she whispered at last. "But bound to you, bound to…" she struggled to find the word "…*debt*."

' "No," I said. "You owe me no obligation, except to go from here before those men come back." She reached out to grasp my arm, pulling me along with her as she hurried away, eager perhaps to remain under my protection. "But why did they bring you out here?" I said to her as we went. "Why would they do such a barbarous thing?"

' "They fear dark spirit in forest," she said. "They fear devil-man."

'I halted in my tracks as I heard these words, which I had long feared I might never hear again. Into my heart there crept a fresh sense of hope. I reached out and grasped her shoulders, looking into her eyes.

' "You are a child of this forest," I said to her. "Tell me now if you know where this devil is said to dwell. The place that he haunts." She gave no reply, but I was certain I saw my answer hidden in her eyes. "You must take me there," I told her. "You must."

'For the first time I saw a look of fear creep upon her. Perhaps she merely grew alarmed by my sudden and frantic change of manner, yet I believed it was something more than that. She firmly shook her head in refusal. "Catia," I said. "I would not ask this of you were it not a thing which means more to me than life itself. You have said you owe me a debt for your life, and this is the only way for you to repay it."

'She stood a while longer in her doubt and indecision, before finally she gave a reluctant nod and replied:

' "You come. I show."

'We walked for a time, the flame from the torch our only light within the utter blackness under the forest canopy. But at length we came to a wide clearing, and I saw the night sky, streaked with thin grey clouds beneath a faint spread of twinkling stars. Then we were climbing a long and meandering pathway up the slope of a wooded hill, whose incline grew steeper as we went. I could sense Catia's gathering disquiet in the deep stillness and silence, and slowly I came to know this sensation within myself, for the night began to feel ever more strange to me as we went higher, and the chill in the air increased. All that had long grown despondent in me warned me now against my growing feelings of anticipation, as I reflected that this path would likely lead me to nowhere but the place of a local superstition: some old story of a ghost or goblin in a haunted glade. I had suffered many such disappointments before. But I must pursue them, these legends and bogey tales, for it seemed that they were all my life had become and perhaps now all it would ever be.

'Soon the torch began to flicker and die, so I discarded it. We went onward for a time in the dark until there came the first rays of dawn. Now I began to see that we stood upon a high ridge of land, which with the daylight would soon command imposing views of the forest all around. Here Catia said we must wait, and she crouched down to conceal herself in the high undergrowth, indicating that I should do the same. As the light grew, she pointed into a deep valley below where I saw emerge out of the fading gloom a great skull-like mound of rock, which rose above all the dense vegetation that grew about it. I was filled by a sense of bitter dismay.

' "Is that it?" I said. "That lump of stone is your forest devil?" It seemed the most foolish and laughable superstition I had ever encountered. I rose up, unable to contain my frustration, and began to climb down the steep face of the hill towards it, determined to demonstrate to her that an odd-shaped dome of rock was nothing to be feared. But instantly she ran after me, growing wild with alarm as she called to me in desperate whispers to go no further. I paid no heed, but continued my descent until she rushed forward to fling herself upon me, throwing her arms about me as she pulled me with all her strength into the cover of some high bushes nearby. I found I did not resist her, for I was overcome by sudden and unexpected feelings as she clung to me, and pressed her body to mine. We stood there together, and in her great fear I felt her tremble against me. At once I put my arms about her, obeying an impulse to comfort and protect her that soon became a feeling of strange delight in simply holding her.

'I could hardly remember the last time I had touched another human being. All such desire in me had long been forgotten, sacrificed to other more violent passions. But now the feel of her as she nestled against me brought at once to my troubled soul a sense of calmness and contentment I had forgotten could exist there. And I began to reflect on the common joys of men, and saw how they had always been denied to me. Now I felt only that I did not ever wish to free her from my arms and that this sublime moment might never end.

'But then I felt her body become rigid with terror, while she buried her face in my breast as I heard come from somewhere nearby the sound of softly treading footsteps, and moments later my senses were assailed by the pungent smell of rotting flesh.

'In the half light, from out of the dense foliage which enveloped us, I vaguely saw a figure go past. Over its shoulders it carried a decomposing deer carcass – carrion scavenged from the forest – but although I could not yet see the scavenger clearly, I gained from it immediately an instinctive impression of loathsomeness and deformity. My flesh began to tremble and creep as my hand reached down to clutch at the hilt of my sword. Could it be – dared I hope? – that finally I had found him?

1st Pizza Direct 3
Park House
King Street
Nairn
VAT 743 2917 29
Tel: 01667 456268
www.1stpizzadirect.co.uk
-SHOP-

PRIORITY   PREPAID

Ticket : 56

Jamie Duncan 06/09/2014 19:19:24
THE CUSTOMER
Expected at : 19:34:24

QTY PRODUCT   PRICE(£)

1 Jumbo Haddock Supper   7.95
1 Standard Haddock   4.65

                    Nett £10.67
                    Tax(20%) £2.13
*PREPAID**   Total £12.80
                    CASH £12.80
                    Change £0.00

Thank You.

'I edged forward, peering through the heavy screen of leaves, observing the back of the figure as it trudged away. But then it turned, looking quickly behind it, and in the dimness I gazed momentarily into its face. What I had sensed was true. It was indeed a monster – but not the one I sought.

'Its face was simply bestial, with a wide bulbous nose and thick protrusions of lumpy bone above the eyes. Its features seemed grotesquely irregular, covered all over by a filthy tangle of beard, and the lips were blubbery and swollen. From its eyes there gleamed a look of unremitting savagery. I saw then that its body, hunched down beneath its stinking burden, was quite short, yet broad and massively muscled, and almost naked save for a few tatters of animal skins which hung about it. I stared after it, barely believing what I saw, as it turned and continued on its path down the hill.

'I had sometimes heard tales told of the dwarf men, or the wild men: creatures of incredible ugliness and malignity who inhabited the most remote and secret places in these lands, and who were often said to live in places beneath the ground. Until now I had not believed in them. But as the daylight began to grow, I looked down at the distant dome of rock, and there I saw others slowly appear: all manner of freakish and sinister figures, that moved to the great stone, and looked warily about them before clambering onto it, one by one, then climbing down to its base before they simply disappeared. Then I knew that hidden beneath the rock must lie the entry to their secret cave.

'But soon, in their midst, I saw a figure far taller than the rest, whose disgusting form I could not mistake. It was he – my hated adversary. I froze, and shook in the grip of rage and triumph as I watched him move among those others, who seemed to give way to him as if they regarded his sheer size with a kind of primitive awe or deference. In a moment I watched him descend beneath the earth, and the rest quickly followed.

'Catia and I remained silent, locked together in our close embrace, not daring to move out from our place of concealment until the sun was fully risen and the valley below had long grown still. Finally we emerged and crept away together from that accursed place, while my mind sought to assess the situation.

'Feared and rejected by men, my enemy had incredibly found his place among a company of monsters. But how might I reach him there? His companions looked strong and dangerous, and would doubtless seek to protect him. I cared little for my own life, but I feared that if I launched an attack I would die before I could kill him. And so he would triumph.

'At a safe distance, I turned to Catia and smiled at her. I felt towards her now a warmth and affection, indeed a kinship, deeper than any I had known in my life. So I told her that she was wise and clever and very brave, and now she must consider that her debt to me was fully discharged. But she did not seem convinced of this, and she looked deep into my eyes as she reached out to take my hand.

' "You come with me?" she said. "Live with my people? Be with *me*?"

'Tears sprang into my eyes as I looked down at her. She too had felt it, this powerful unspoken bond between us. And to her, a feral child of the woods, I appeared neither wild nor frightening. I might never have imagined this. For long years I had considered nothing beyond the destruction of my detested sibling. It had filled my mind and driven me onward through unendurable hardship and privation. I had long ago accepted that no other life was possible for me. But now, as if by some miracle, I saw that one was offered. A light broke into my darkness. It seemed at last I had discovered my enemy only to find that he had placed himself beyond my reach. And I was tired… so very tired. Yet even as I saw this, there reached out to me the hand of *freedom*. Might it be so? Could it be that the Fates would finally release me from my dismal burden and grant me a new life, among foreign people, where the shadow of my past could not touch me? I reached out to Catia and held her, brushing my face against her hair, gathering her warmth and softness to me. And in that moment I dared to imagine that I might become human again. That I might be once more a *man*, and live in the company of others, with a wife at my hearth, and children…

'A spear of ice seemed to pierce my heart. I had long told myself bitterly that my mission of retribution was my father's only legacy to me. But I saw now this was not so. There was also his blood – his tainted blood. How could I take a wife and visit this blight upon her? To contaminate her body, her community, her descendants with the blood of monsters. For we had all become freaks and monsters: my father, my brother, and me. I flung her from me, and cried out:

' "Go back to your people. I cannot go with you. I am cursed. *I am cursed!*"

'I turned and ran blindly until I was far away. Then I fell to the ground and screamed out my desolation into the empty skies. I was condemned to be forever alone – the Fates had decreed it so. Then my cries turned into mad laughter as I thought of that despicable wretch who was my brother and saw again the grim and tragic joke: that truly we had grown to become much alike. Twin souls, Urta had said. But he had always been the dominant one. He had stolen my life and afterwards governed my existence: forever in front, leading me and taunting me.

But now there had grown a great disparity between us. For he had found companionship of his own monstrous sort. He had achieved fellowship and belonging, while I could have none! And my hatred for him swelled beyond reason.

'Now I saw what I must do to reach him. I must somehow enlist the aid of others. Armed and prepared, we must enter that hellish underground place to destroy a nest of monsters.

'I rose up, and as I made my way through the forest, I cut at intervals signs upon the trees. I went for many hours, marking my route in this way, until I came to a wide track where the woods had been cleared. I followed this until I reached the edge of the forest. Soon I came to the hall of the local lord, an old Roman fort surrounded by a decayed defensive wall: a square-shaped structure built from crumbling stone, shored and supported all over with pieces of wooden framework.

'As I approached the entrance the guards came out to surround me. They did not understand me, but regarded me fearfully as they jabbered at me in Celtic and pointed their spears at me. But I submitted myself to them, laying down my sword, and at last they took me inside, shutting me in a dark cell in a dungeon below the ground. They gave me food and water, looking upon me as a great curiosity, and I languished there for a time before the lord himself came to view this oddity, this wodewose from the forest. There also came with him his son, a boy upon the brink of manhood. A youth named Cadroc.'

Chapter Fifteen

The man called Cynewulf fell silent and fixed his eyes on Brother Cadroc. Yet the monk did not return his look, but only gazed far out into the distance, while his face appeared much troubled. At last Cynewulf turned to Aelfric and me, and said:

'So it was that we set out to pursue those devils, to corner them in their lair, where the chanting of the monks defeated them, and I came at last to face my hated foe and take my longed-for revenge upon him as the cave collapsed and I drove my blade deep into his heart. Perhaps you have heard these things related by Cadroc? But this is not the end of my story.

'When I emerged from out of the cave, I departed immediately from the company of Cadroc and the others, slipping away easily amidst all the uproar and confusion. I needed to be alone with my thoughts, to come to terms with the great complexity of my emotions. At first there resided in me only a kind of numbness, a sense of disbelief that finally it was over. But this gave way gradually to feelings I could not have anticipated. There grew in my heart no swell of triumph or exultation, but rather a deep melancholy, almost a sensation of grief akin to what I had felt at the loss of my old life. I imagined I understood this: that the singular compulsion which for years had ruled my existence was suddenly gone, as if I had awoken from a long and incredible dream. But in all those years I had never paused to think beyond its accomplishment. Now that it was done, and my arch-enemy dead, I must come to terms with the realisation that I was finally and utterly alone in the world, without direction or purpose. What I felt was indeed a sense of loss. Yet I soon began to understand that it was something far more.

'For he began to haunt me. Wherever I went I could not escape him. In death his ghost pursued me as in life I pursued him. I started to sense his presence, and the feeling of him grew ever more powerful as I began to hear his footsteps following mine like an echo; and I would turn to see nothing but *know* he was there. I would hear his sighs upon the wind and the sound of him as he crept beyond my sight among the trees and rushes. Then I began to see him! At dawn or dusk, standing far out in the mist, waiting and watching, his image at first only a blur that almost imperceptibly grew stronger and more distinct until finally the clear vision of him took form before me, exactly as I saw him in his last living moments before I struck the fatal blow. Because in that instant I had seen in his eyes only a look of rage, fear and confusion. It was then I understood that he did not recognise or remember me – that he did not know me at all, that I meant exactly nothing to him. He did not understand the reason for his death. There was only a dull glare of brute incomprehension. But over the years he had grown in my mind to become my consummate enemy. I came to see in him every aspect of malice and cunning as he outwitted and eluded me in our duel to the death. I saw a monster of iniquity, my mortal foe, motivated by devilish spite. Yet I realised at the end that in truth he was none of these things, but only a desperate, wretched and despised outcast – a victim who had sought simply to survive. Finally I understood him and that all the hate and vindictiveness I came to see in him had all along been truly my own. Now I remembered the last words that Urta spoke as she saw her vision of a monster: "Beware it, for it is yourself, and your hatred will make it *deadly!*"

'So finally I saw the reality of it – how my father's madness had likewise come to be my own. But now there came also my father's demon of self-horror and despair. I came to the Fens as an outcast, and since then I have existed here alone… and yet never alone. *He* has been forever with me like a distorted mirror image, his outward deformity the perfect reflection of my inward corruption.

'But then, a short time ago, I began to have the dream. It is the same vision I suffered on the battlefield in my youth. It has returned to me. Each night the crows come, flocking obscenely upon me, covering me with their crawling horror. I seem to feel myself rise from my bed, yet I cannot wake or break free. And I imagine I stumble far out onto the fen, and still the birds swarm about me and cling to me, cloaking me with their blackness as I draw my sword and strike at them in desperate fury. Until suddenly I understand that they are *his* creatures – that his time has come, and now it is he who moves against *me*. This is surely what the dream portends.

'Yet now the dream changes, and I find myself stalking through the dark, creeping with silent intent upon a lonely cottage which stands in the distance ahead, somewhere on the border of the marshes. Pale moonlight shines behind me as I move ever more swiftly and feel within me the gathering of both a monstrous rage and a terrible joy. I come to stand at the shadowed doorway of the hut, then smash at it so the timber breaks and splinters, and I see inside the faint glowing embers of the hearth and the dark huddled shapes which rise from sleep in alarm and terror. And my heart burns with sheer hate at the sight of the warmth and life and kinship they share. I move in among them, see dimly their faces, male and female, young and old, and my fury grows as I see the horror in their eyes when they look upon me. And I breathe in their helpless fear to make me stronger as I strike at them and feel the tear of flesh, the spatter of blood and the crunch of bone as they fall. And still I strike, pounding and crushing them into the dust until their screams and sobs are silenced forever.

'In moments I turn and rush back into the night, for I know that the night is mine, and I feel my spirit exult in wicked triumph at the death and destruction I have wrought, as the darkness closes upon me and the dream slowly fades…'

He paused for a moment, his head sinking down as he gave a deep sigh. Then he went on: 'The dreams started as I heard whispers out in the fens that a murderous demon had risen to stalk this land. Then I learned that a man called Cadroc had come to use Christian magic against this dark one – and I knew at once what the Fates had decreed. So I set out to follow your path. Now you know my story. And you must guide my steps from here.'

He looked at Cadroc with expectation, but the monk barely seemed to have heard his last words, yet appeared to be lost deep in his thoughts, until at last he turned to Cynewulf uneasily while he began to shake his head.

'Lord Cynewulf,' he said, 'your tale is most remarkable. But what you have told me greatly disturbs me. These long years I have never once doubted that what you confronted in that cave was a demonic thing from Hell. It has been the very bedrock of my faith. But now you tell me it was really just a man? That those devils we fought were only degraded examples of humanity?'

'Yes!' Cynewulf answered. 'But do not doubt that what we face now is something much worse.'

Cadroc looked back at him in confusion, but at once I understood the import of these grim words, and I said:

'Lord Cynewulf suggests that his twin has become a vengeful spirit.' It was clear to me this was his heathen belief. Yet even as my mind tried to dismiss the notion, my heart shuddered at it.

'Twin souls?' Cynewulf whispered. 'Or a single soul torn and divided? The spirits of those monsters are trapped forever inside the cave which became their tomb. Only he among them remains connected to the living world, and he carries within him the power of all their rage. This connection between us is powerful, our life-force shared. I took his life, but he returned to haunt my mind and infest my soul, until finally in death he has become the implacable enemy I supposed him to be in life. Truly he has become my dark *fetch*. He draws on my vital energy to take earthly form and revenge himself upon the world of men. He sends to me a challenge, and there must be a last reckoning between us. Once more I must confront him and dispatch him into the realm of the dead. But how? How may a man fight a dark spirit? A wrathful ghost? I do not fear any mortal foe, but *this…*' At once a great terror seemed to overcome him, and he struggled visibly to contain it. Then he said to Cadroc: 'This is why I come to you. I saw inside that cave the power of your Christian magic, which brought great rocks crashing down onto the heads of our enemies to consign them to the underworld. From here on I go with you. Our paths are made one, and once more we must stand and fight him together.'

'The power of my God is great,' Cadroc answered distantly. 'But your story has made me doubt my own power. I am no longer certain of the truth of these things!'

It was clear to me now as I looked at Cadroc how deeply Cynewulf's revelations had shaken his self-confidence and perhaps even his faith. That ironically he had begun to doubt his own certainty of a supernatural agency at work even as Cynewulf came entirely to believe in one. New seeds of doubt were growing in my own mind. What we faced was something brutal and deadly, but if it were a thing entirely of the physical world, then might mere words and symbols – however holy – prevail against it? I saw now that from the start it had been Cadroc's great faith, his unflinching zeal and courage in his cause, which had carried me with him. It was upon him I had fixed my own hope of salvation in my struggle against the darkness. But now Cadroc's doubts became also mine, as I began to consider the awful possibility that we were not here as the spiritual warriors of God, but only as men who were filled hopelessly with false pride and self-deceit. And the dismal expanse of the wilderness all around seemed at once to overshadow us, to reduce us to insignificance and grow more hostile and threatening with each passing moment.

There was also within me an unnerving feeling that there were aspects of Cynewulf's story which held some strange significance or parallel to my own, but it was all unclear, and somehow I could not find the sense of it. But something else troubled me. I remembered Aelfric's words to me earlier suggesting that Cynewulf himself might be the murderer. While I did not suspect Cynewulf's integrity, I wholly doubted his mental fortitude as I saw how his old obsession still entirely dominated him, his mind even now fixated upon his dead brother. I had once heard a story from a visitor to the monastery about a man who suffered a head wound, and then became afflicted by dark moods and fits of rage which afterwards he could not recall – as if two separate spirits or personalities had come incredibly to coexist inside him. The older monks had hastened to assure me the story was merely fanciful, but I was beginning to question whether the Church was always right about the things it lightly dismissed – like the existence of the wild men. In this place it became easier to believe such tales. I was suddenly shocked by the possibility that a man as disturbed and inwardly conflicted as Cynewulf could be a killer without having any memory or consciousness of it. My mind was a cloud of confusion, and I no longer knew what to think or believe about anything.

As these things ran through my thoughts, I felt something deep and fearful begin to stir in me. Then my eyes fell shut as it seemed I recalled once more my vision during the shaman's ritual: that in my mind I stood in the glow of firelight, returned to the night-land beyond my hermitage, looking upward as I witnessed the stealthy approach of that terrible giant figure. Once again I saw it step out of the shadows and into the flickering light, and I was seized by the fearful knowledge that in moments my memory of it would be restored, and I would look upon its face…

It stood before me, and as its features found form I felt its eyes upon me. I froze with the terrible certainty that now *I knew what it was*…

My eyes opened and I gave a gasp, struggling in my mind to keep hold of the image. But already it was gone, slipping away like sand between my fingers, and again I could remember only the form of a thing huge and swathed in darkness. Aelfric had noticed my disturbed state and came at once to my side to lay a reassuring hand on my shoulder.

'My memory of the marauder!' I told him. 'It started to return. For a moment it seemed to grow clear. But now it is lost again.'

'It was perhaps not a memory but a foreseeing,' he said gravely – his resilient cheerfulness was now a thing of the past. 'All will soon be revealed to us. We are passing now into the most deep and remote parts of the Fenlands. It is a secret place of great mystery and power, which is said to stand as a gateway to the spirit world itself. Here our reckoning with this dark one must surely come.'

Whatever the truth of this, it was plainly true that – *like Cynewulf* – something haunted me from within, which struggled to rise up and break free: a thing blacker than night, that followed me 'as a demon in the dark', and it felt strangely as if I were fleeing from it even as we pursued it. It seemed suddenly that the whole grim saga of Cynewulf and Cadroc had risen like a monster to swallow me whole – to join the threads of all our stories into one.

As we moved on, our pace slowed, while the day grew heavy and humid, and the clouds gathered and glowered overhead colouring the sky with deep vibrant hues of purplish grey. The marshes grew ever more wild and dispiriting, and our progress became increasingly laborious. While we trudged along a pathway around a wide stinking stretch of sunken ground filled with foul stagnant water, where great swarms of gnats formed a floating haze above its surface, I looked before me at the compact figure of Aelfric as he walked beside the towering one of the old warrior.

'I wish I had been born into the warrior's caste,' I heard Aelfric say with feeling. 'It is the life I would have chosen.'

'You have a brave soul, young friend,' Cynewulf answered. 'It shines in you. But do not confuse your ideals with reality.

Warriors are not as you imagine them. They are only men who condition themselves to be what they are by a code of swagger and bluster. Many spend their lives so drunk that much of the time they can barely tell one end of a sword from another. It is fear that rules such men. And all their vows of duty are only the words they speak to hide from the truth of themselves – justifications for doing things which in their hearts they know to be wrong.'

For some reason as we journeyed onward these words remained with me, as I felt an ever-growing sense of disquiet.

Later in the afternoon Aelfric informed us that we were approaching one of the few settlements in this sparsely inhabited region. It was part of his and Cadroc's duty to visit all the local villages to check upon their safety and warn of the danger – for these places were so isolated and remote that it was possible the people had not yet heard news of it – and since it was growing late Aelfric proposed we should pass the night there. I supposed it was Cadroc's intention to move about among the few local settlements in the expectation that our presence would soon coincide with a new attack. But I did not ask him this, for his manner had grown most distant and withdrawn.

Soon we came to the village – the place was called Sceaf's ford – standing upon small elevations of fertile land close to a wide stream in the middle of the marsh: a group of dilapidated huts which crouched almost hidden behind the trees. On its outskirts Cynewulf held back, sitting down suddenly to conceal himself among the high reeds.

'I will remain here and keep watch!' he declared to us.

'You mean to stay out here alone all night?' I said, as renewed feelings of suspicion towards him rose in me.

'It is the life I have come to know,' he answered simply.

'My presence will unsettle those villagers. Do not fear. None shall see me – I will cause no alarm. I will be vigilant and at one with the darkness. I carry food and water with me.'

As we turned to leave him I asked myself: upon whom does he mean to keep watch?

'I think it is also the presence of others which unsettles him,' Aelfric whispered to me. 'And what is wrong with Brother Cadroc?' I looked back at him and frowned, as I saw that he shared my own uneasy feeling at Cynewulf's self-imposed presence among us, along with a sense that our company had begun to drift into a state of fearful uncertainty.

'I will speak with Cadroc,' I said. 'Later.'

'Good!' he nodded. 'His task is hardest of all, and for it he must be strong. It is for both of us, in our different ways, to support him and keep his purpose true.'

We came to the village and called out to make our approach known. From amongst the huts and trees curious faces emerged to peer out at us. Several men then approached us, their manner seeming cautious and taciturn, and I saw at once what Cadroc had meant when he said these marsh dwellers were more wild and primitive than the Gyrwas folk we had so far encountered. Their long hair was tied up to stand like plumes on the tops of their heads, and they wore many necklaces made from bones and animal teeth. They openly displayed pagan talismans, including the symbol of Thunor's hammer, which was like an inverted cross. There was something backward and clannish about these men that made me uncomfortable in their presence, and I did not care at all for the prospect of spending the night here. We were taken to the house of the head-man, whose name was Huda – a bulky, fierce-looking individual whose hard stare I found most intimidating. He listened to our words then nodded to indicate that he was already aware of the terror which threatened the land, then said he would allocate to us a barn in which we might sleep. We were then given food from his hearth – a stew of eels which I felt I must sample as an act of courtesy while I ate some barley-bread – served up to us by a pale-faced girl.

In the corner of the room there sat a boy – perhaps Huda's son – who paid us little attention but was constantly busy with a knife, carving at a block of wood. While we ate I watched his carving start to take shape as he worked with great dexterity and speed, and it came to depict a kind of hideous scowling face – I presumed a representation of one of their devil-gods. After a time he looked up to notice my interest and gave me a wide grin, saying:

'It is Tiw, our protector. I carve many such to put up in houses all around our village. To scare away the evil spirit.'

'It is skilfully done,' I told him, mindful that it was our mission here to attempt to convert the heathens, 'but it will give you no protection.' I reached inside my robe and brought out my cross. 'Here is the symbol of my God – the one true God – which will defend you against evil. You should carve this image to protect yourselves.'

'The one God?' he said with a bewildered look. 'Our gods are many, but their *spirit* is one – the Great Spirit of which everything in creation is a part. The gods we serve are all born of the Great Spirit. They are His children.'

'No!' I tried to explain. 'There is only one God, who is God the Father, God the Son and God the Holy Spirit…'

'So you have three gods who are all of one spirit?' he replied. 'Yes – that is like us, except we have more gods. This is what I have said to you.'

With child-like sincerity he spoke to me as if I were a child who failed to understand something very simple, but his words defeated me, for I could find no easy answer to them. He stared at my cross and smiled at me again as he went back to his carving, and I felt then how deeply I had become lost within these lonely wastelands, where all my life's certainties seemed to slip somewhere far beyond my reach. Dismayed and perplexed, I looked to Cadroc, expecting his help, but none came. He merely sat, evidently preoccupied, silent and absorbed in his thoughts. Then he rose and left us to go to rest. Seeing my chance to speak with him alone, I too excused myself, leaving Aelfric to sit talking with Huda, and the girl led me outside and directed me to our place of lodging. As I walked there I looked beyond the village, out into the gathering darkness, and my thoughts turned to Cynewulf, alone in the night. At once, beyond all my doubtful feelings towards him, it seemed that I understood him better, indeed shared almost an odd kind of kinship with him, as I feared that I too had become like an outsider who was awkward and ill at ease in the society of others. But still Cynewulf's presence disturbed me.

I entered the barn to find Cadroc sitting inside, staring despondently into the flame of a rush candle, then went to sit beside him, and said:

'What are your feelings about Cynewulf? His mind is clearly unsound. Can we be sure of him? Are you content to let him join us?'

'I cannot deny him!' he answered, looking up at me sharply. 'No man alive could have greater right or cause to stand with me. And yet his story...' his voice trailed back into melancholy silence. I nodded, as I saw it was not my place to dispute with him in this. So I went on:

'It is clear to me how conflicted you have become. That is something I might never have expected to see in you.'

'What if I have been wrong?' he said suddenly in an

agonised tone, his eyes gaping as they reflected the light of the dancing yellow flame. 'All these years I have believed... but what if I have been wrong and my mission is not God's will but only my wicked pride and conceit? My own reckless presumption – a deception of the Devil!'

'You have not been wrong,' I told him, no doubt seeking to convince myself as much as Cadroc. 'Surely it is God's intention that we should sometimes come to question our faith? This is what makes the triumph of faith more glorious. But we must hold fast to our beliefs. Long ago inside that cave you witnessed the power of God bring down destruction on His enemies – whether they were demons or men it does not matter. Remember also that it is your object in this mission to bring Christian truth to these pagans and save their foolish souls. How can this be other than God's will?'

It appeared that my words had touched him, for something seemed to gather and strengthen within him, while a spark of his old determination and zeal returned into his eyes even as he looked at me.

'Of course you are right,' he agreed. 'I will reflect on what you have said. You have helped to reassure me, Brother. This is not the time to lose heart.' Then he gazed deep into my eyes and smiled. 'I always supposed God sent you to me for a purpose.'

Now it was I who sought to find comfort in his words. I spent a restless night, but it passed without disturbance, and in the morning I was happy to leave that miserable village. But I was encouraged as we departed to see that Cadroc appeared much restored to his normal resolute self, as I saw how deeply my own state of mind had come to depend upon his. As we distanced ourselves from Sceaf's ford, I looked about to see that Cynewulf had silently reappeared to walk at our side. And so our journey continued.

It was later in the day that there crept over Cynewulf an air of uneasy alertness as he began to cast looks about the silent stretches of empty fens surrounding us.

'There is a strong sense in me that we are watched,' he said quietly. 'That we do not walk here alone.' His words at first did not worry me unduly. I had known this same feeling ever since I set out onto the marshes and supposed it to be only a natural deception of the mind in a place so bleak and lonely. But Cynewulf was accustomed to travelling in these Fenlands, and so I began to wonder if it might be foolish to disregard his concern. Then he said to Cadroc: 'Our enemy lies low for now. But soon the time will come. Then your spells will defeat him, and together we will send him into the death-lands forever.'

Now Cadroc turned to Aelfric and said:

'Where is it we are headed?'

'To my home,' Aelfric replied. 'Tonight we stay with my own people and will receive warm welcome.'

'Are there other settlements along the way that we must visit?' Cadroc asked.

'There is one,' Aelfric said. 'Local men call it the Isle of the Dead. Do not let its name alarm you. It is called so after the many old death mounds which stand thereabouts.' He fell silent for several moments before he added: 'It is the place where I was born.'

'Aelfric,' I said, 'you should not go there. There are bad memories for you…'

'I must go,' he answered. 'Others who are kin to me live there now, and their welfare is my duty. The marshes around the island are most dangerous, even to those who know them if mists should come. You must not attempt the journey without me to guide you. Do not worry. It will be well for me.'

The atmosphere grew stifling as the day progressed, while the grey monotony of the way ahead appeared to me like a hidden pathway deep into a forgotten world – to the last earthly refuge of something old and terrible which existed here far beyond the light of God. As we passed finally into the dark heart of this land, my feelings fell again into a deep and powerful imagining that it was the ancient ways that still held sway here, and that now it was the Fates which spun their unseen strands to encompass us and drive our steps ineluctably onward into the lost domain of our enemy – the Great Spirit of the pagans, which had been revered since time immemorial as a god in the hearts of my people, but was now cast down to become something vengeful and monstrous: a fallen angel transformed into a malevolent devil. Soon the veil would be torn aside, and it would come in some frightful form to face us – we who came in the name of the Church to invade its stronghold – in a final clash between light and darkness. These images came to haunt my mind, and my anxiety began to grow as I now became slowly aware of distant sounds which called out across the wetlands. Remote, chilling cries drifted almost imperceptibly upon the air and seemed to resonate in some deep and barely conscious part of me, like a voice that whispered secretly into the farthest reaches of my soul. My nerves grew taut as gradually this awareness increased. Until Aelfric suddenly pointed into the distance and announced:

'We are approaching the island. You must follow close behind me as we draw near and not stray from my path. There are many hidden mud pools, very deep. We must tread with great care.'

To our west, perhaps half a league away, and enveloped by a grey haze of thin mist, lay the Isle of the Dead. As we drew closer to it, the faraway sound slowly gained in clarity, until at last I knew what it was I heard. It was a great gathering of cawing crows. Cynewulf gasped out as he too realised this, and I turned to see that his face had grown ashen.

'Something is wrong here!' Aelfric cried, abandoning his caution and beginning to run across the waterlogged ground. We hurried to keep pace with him, all of us following in his footsteps, our feet sinking into the mud as the low, creeping mist began to seep about us. Now I saw the island more clearly ahead, a wide circle of land dotted with trees which loomed eerily against the heavy sky. Our path took us past several small islets where stood some of those earthen burial mounds which gave the place its name. Then I saw the crows: the ominous sight of numerous birds as they sat on the claw-like branches of the trees. But I saw no other signs of life.

In the middle of the island stood several buildings: dwellings and outhouses. In his desperation Aelfric rushed straight to the door of the largest of these, then stopped outside, caution at once overtaking him. Cadroc and I came to stand beside him, and Cadroc drew his sword while Aelfric raised his spear, as we then became aware that a strange, rank odour permeated the air. Then there came a sound: a faint but distinct scratching or scuffling noise from inside. We stood tense as Aelfric sprang forward to fling open the door.

From the dimness within there was an instant stirring of frenzied motion, and my heart squirmed then seemed about to burst as a thing of unutterable horror, scrambling and shapeless, rose up at me in a waft of stinking foulness that felt half solid as it smothered and clung to me. For a moment my senses nearly failed as my consciousness was assailed by a screaming mass of living fury amidst a wild flurry of clawing blackness. An enraged scream split the air, then I heard my own voice shriek out in my dread, echoing up into the louring sky.

196

At last my stunned mind began to make sense of this erupting chaos. From out of the hut there came at us a furious swarm of flying insects, and the thrashing wings of crows as they launched themselves towards us and out through the door. Inside the air was clogged with black clouds of flies, while more of the filthy birds flapped away to escape through a rear door which hung half open on shattered hinges. The cry had come from Aelfric as he looked inside, and as my sight grew clear I saw there in the gloom a vision of ultimate monstrosity. Propped up into sitting positions around the walls, and placed in a circle around the central hearth in what was like the insane replication of a living scene, were the mangled and gore soaked corpses of an entire family – men, women and children. The decaying flesh on their faces was pecked bloody and raw, and their eyeholes gaped black and empty, picked clean by the scavenging birds. I stood and stared blankly as I felt bile burning in my throat, but I could not move, for I was simply numb with disbelief. Once more the Isle of the Dead had become a place true to its name.

Aelfric reeled away while Cadroc staggered backwards and cried out:

'By God and all the saints, this is a sacrilege no man could conceive. A diseased mockery of hearth and home and fellowship. *It is a vile desecration of life itself!'*

And so it was. I could never have imagined anything like this – this foul inversion of all that was natural and good. It was like a deed of deranged hatred against the whole of humankind. I stumbled away from it, then saw that Cynewulf stood motionless in the shadows nearby, his body rigid as he gazed transfixed at the obscenity in the hut. All around us I felt the sinister eyes of the roosting crows, like the omni-present stare of a single pervading consciousness. Aelfric had fallen to the ground, and I saw that grief and horror were rendering him overcome and insensible.

'I know what we must do!' Cadroc called out to me, his eyes becoming almost crazed. 'This charnel house must be burned to the ground. Let purifying flame destroy and obliterate it totally.'

His words roused us both to something like madness: an outraged and unthinking need simply to act. We broke into the nearby shelters, ripping out timber and straw, then Cadroc struck together flint and iron to raise sparks which grew into flame. In one of the huts we discovered a supply of torches, and as our bonfire rose we took and lighted some of these, and ran into the surrounding structures, setting fire to wood and thatch. Finally Cadroc strode to the main hut to hurl a torch in among the ravaged corpses, and the polluted air ignited suddenly as the roof burst into flames.

The fire quickly grew and spread until soon the whole settlement was a roaring inferno. Cadroc and I watched in silence as it burned, and as I stood a dull feeling came over me, my mind seeming once more to become lost within a sense of creeping unreality. For in the marshes all around us, thick patches of mist were rising as the twilight began to fall, and I realised now that our path away from the island would not be safe until morning. We were trapped here for the night, and soon the darkness would come.

Chapter Sixteen

I knelt beside Aelfric, who lay curled up and motionless on the grass, then I spoke his name and placed my hand on his arm, as if to awaken him from his stupor. Slowly he looked up at me, but he was deep in a state of shock, his eyes blank and empty as he began to gasp and tremble, sinking beyond my reach into the darkest places of his mind before he whispered:

'Death is here. All are lost. I cannot help them!' It appeared to me as if the gruesome scenes of slaughter and fire on this island had cast his mind back into the terrors of his childhood, those memories rising to claw him down and devastate him. Then a frightful thought came to me. Our wild impulse to burn the blasphemy in the hut had been uncontrollable, but now I saw how the fire would have served as a beacon for many miles throughout these flatlands. If our enemy were out there – he would have seen. Now Cadroc lit a fresh torch and turned from the blaze, his voice growing harsh as he called out:

'I cannot delay. My work must begin.' He strode away, and unthinking I rose to follow him, drawn by his firm look of purpose. 'Soon the darkness will rise!' he thundered. 'I feel it is coming. But mine is the knowledge and the power to defeat it. *To drive it back!*'

He led me to where the land bordered the marsh, standing his torch upright in the ground and driving its shaft down into the earth. Then he took out his book of arcane rites, along with a small goatskin pouch tied with a cord. From this he emptied a collection of tiny objects, and I saw that they were fragments of bone and human teeth. 'Relics of the saints,' he said to me. 'Objects of great holiness and power.' Under his breath he began to utter chants in Latin, which then lapsed into Celtic as he placed these things on the bank in a circular pattern around the torch, so that its light spread out to fill the circle as Cadroc came finally to stand inside it, while he clutched fiercely at the metal cross on his breast. Next he held up the book in both hands, as he threw back his head and cried out: 'Though I walk through the valley of the shadow of death, I will fear no evil! With the Lord at my side I do not fear. I shall overcome... I shall...' He fell to his knees, and his body began to shake violently as his eyes rolled back into his head until I could see only the whites of them. His voice was gabbling now, spittle flying from his lips as he croaked out more words from the psalms. 'I am filled with burning... and without strength in my flesh... I am utterly spent and overcome... I groan at the tumult in my heart... O God! Do not forsake me. The darkness rises... it comes for me. Do not let it prevail against me!'

I looked upon these ravings with growing horror, as I realised that what at first had seemed to be religious fervour was in truth a mounting hysteria – that Cadroc's great crisis of faith had returned to reach its breaking point, and in this desperate hour of trial he had come to doubt both himself and God. He appeared to be on the very brink of insanity. I knew then that what he fought here was not the darkness outside, but truly a great conflict within himself: a struggle against a spiralling fear and madness in his own soul. It was a condition horribly familiar to me, yet in him it was suddenly more violent and extreme than anything I could have imagined. A sense of hopelessness now desolated me, as I knew that without Cadroc we were surely lost.

I turned away from him while his frenetic wails rose up over the shadowy wetlands, and my brain grew inert with the sense of disbelief as I looked out over the marshes and the dusk deepened. It seemed to me then that there came strange sounds from beyond: distant murmurings and stirrings from the swaying reeds and shifting mud, echoing the fearful things which rose inside my mind. Then I froze, as far out in the greying haze I saw sudden movement, a distant glimmer of dull light that shone for a moment and then was gone. But in a few moments I saw it again: the eerie glow of an unnatural brightness that drifted wisp-like into the mist, then flared up like a lantern in the seething vapours above the bogs in what was like the swirling motions of a wild spectral dance. And gradually I felt sure it was approaching us, while I gazed upon it motionless and enthralled.

Desperately I now sought to take control of myself and turned to flee back to the smoking remains of the huts. I looked down at Aelfric, who lay sprawled and unmoving on the ground where I had left him, and I knew with despair that I must find some way to return him and Cadroc to their senses. In panic I turned towards Cynewulf, who still stood gazing deep into the crimson glow of the ruined structures, his sword drawn and clutched tightly to his breast like a symbol of religious consolation. All my doubts and fears concerning Cynewulf's state of mind returned in a moment as I remembered him as the raging unbalanced creature who had attacked me in the fog. I feared again the possibility that the dark spirit he pursued lay truly within him – that hidden inside the man there might dwell a monster. I now felt a deep certainty that he had brought some black spell or curse upon our company. But I also knew that Cynewulf was my last and only hope.

As I approached him, he did not turn to look at me, but I saw his eyes glow bright red as he fixed them into the dying firelight. Then he spoke in a tone that was flat and strange, and I knew at once that some awful change had crept upon him.

'Cadroc has failed!' he said with a hollow, desolate laugh. 'Listen to him raving into the night. He has lost and his magic has failed. It is over.'

There was something so remote and disturbing in his manner, as he stood there stiff and glassy-eyed, that it seemed he was no longer like himself. But how could I know this truly when I understood so little of the man, yet feared so much?

'Did you see the omen of the crows?' he said, his voice a cold whisper. 'Little black harbingers of death. They speak to me. The gods speak to me. They tell me he is coming – coming with the darkness – and retribution will be his. His will be the final victory. He will tear out and devour my soul. He will claim it at last for his own!'

At once his strength appeared to crumble as his legs gave way, and he slumped down onto the earth while his great body began to quake and shudder as he gasped for breath, and I looked in horrified incredulity at the sight of this grizzled giant who seemed in a moment to become like a terrified child. Then I knew that as Aelfric had succumbed to his memories, and Cadroc to his doubts, so Cynewulf now fell prey to his own deepest fear – his dread of things supernatural. But there was something terrible about him that chilled my blood, as his eyes bulged and his teeth chattered – a sense that what came over him was something more than simply fear.

I shook my head hopelessly, for I saw that he too was lost to me, and I understood the shocking truth that all my companions had fallen deep into their own gulfs of terror, which gaped beneath them as the darkness fell. And now I stood alone – alone upon the brink of my soul's own darkness as I faced the approaching night. I moved away reaching inside my robe and drawing out my cross, but it seemed now to bring me little comfort. Then I felt my senses sharpen as I trained them into the crepuscular shadows ahead, while tremors of sheer dread began to fill my heart. For I became aware with sudden certainty that something moved out there beyond the scope of my sight, a thing of infinite stealth that crept slowly but inexorably towards me. With a trembling hand I raised up my cross and sought desperately in my mind for commands to hold back the thing that approached, but the words merely faltered and died on my lips as my breath rose in harsh groans, and my breast throbbed agonisingly, while the pulse in my temples pounded a frantic rhythm into my brain as I felt the last of my faith and strength seep away to desert me. Helplessly I watched as a tall shape cloaked in darkness began to take form before me, and I could not move or cry out but only stand powerless as the dreadful visitant advanced into the glow of the distant firelight. I did not know if what I felt most was terror or relief as I stared into the face of the shaman Taeppa.

The shaman stamped his staff down onto the earth, then looked from under his raven-feathered hat at my outstretched cross, and said:

'When the evil comes – and I sense that it will – you must find a stronger defence than *that*!' He turned his head slightly, towards the sound of Cadroc's frenzied ranting, and remarked: 'Is this your Christian miracle of resurrection? You make enough noise to raise the dead?' I remained speechless as he looked back at me. 'I have been with you on your journey from Meretun. I knew I would not be welcome among your company. But I was aware that the time might come when I should be needed.'

I gaped at him in confusion, fearful of him from our previous encounter, yet also comforted by the mere fact of another human presence. At once I gave a cry, my nerves close to breaking as I gestured out into the blackness of the fen, where I saw once more a sudden flaring of that macabre glowing light. The shaman looked towards it and nodded.

'Phantoms of the marsh,' he said, as my eyes followed the uncanny sight. 'They walk deep in the swamps where it is not safe for mortals to go. Do not let your look be drawn to them. They will cast an enchantment on a man and lead him to certain death.'

I tore my eyes away. It seemed there was no end to the horrors in this place.

Now the shaman moved past me, looking down at the stricken figures of Cynewulf and Aelfric.

'Our situation is fearful,' I began to babble. 'The inhabitants of this island are all murdered, and a terrible madness has fallen upon my companions...'

'Fear has overcome them,' the shaman said grimly, 'because they do not know the true nature of the thing they must confront. Only that, whether man or spirit, our enemy is indeed a monster who weaves a web of fear to entangle us, to make us weak and divided, each trapped alone within his soul's worst terror. We must learn what it is we face and whether to fight it foremost with spear or spell. To know this will restore and unite us. It will focus and strengthen us against the great dread of what is unknown.' He looked at me closely with his piercing gaze. 'There is only one way to achieve this. We must do now what was left unfinished at Meretun.' I stared at him as my heart began to tremble. 'I must cast a memory spell, and you must journey within yourself to uncover the truth that is hidden there. The darkness must be drawn forth. To look into the past is our way to see into the future.'

'I cannot do this!' I told him. 'With my friends incapable, I must stay alert to watch over them...'

'To what avail?' he said. 'So you may see sooner when death approaches?'

Fear and suspicion began to crackle in my brain. How might I trust the word of a pagan wizard? I recalled too well his sinister powers of entrancement. It might even be that he was himself an agent of the Devil, who would perform some blasphemous ritual or spell to summon the monster for his own wicked purpose. Every manner of wild and fantastic imagining came flooding into my head. But what choice did I have? I saw finally that his words were irresistible – that the key to this matter lay somewhere inside my mind, and finally I must turn to face it, to try to break this strange malediction which had fallen upon us. For the sake of us all I must place my faith in this man. Now he approached me, flinging off his hat and throwing down the leather bag which hung from a strap over his shoulder, then drawing up his knife as he had done back in Meretun, moving it to and fro in gentle swaying motions as he brought it before my eyes.

'Let that which is lost be found!' he pronounced. 'What you see in the spirit lands will be terrifying. But do not let your courage fail!'

In the distant light of our bonfire, I gazed upon the faintly glowing blade as the shaman leaned close to me, his body moving rhythmically from side to side as a faint humming sound began to rise in his throat until it welled into a high-pitched drone that filled his head. Again he drew his blade so near to my face that my sight was a blur, and my eyes closed as his voice rose in a sonorous tone which seemed to drown out the far-off ravings of Cadroc. It felt to me then as if I embarked upon some awful passage of initiation.

'Return now in your mind to the spirit-shrine where we met, see it clearly in every detail, and remember those things that passed there between us. Recall the feelings you knew in those moments.' The image grew vividly in my brain, as I knew a momentary reawakening of the alarm and then the strange irreconcilable emotions I had experienced. Then softly he continued: 'Now your mind will expand to embrace all that is within and what lies beyond. Deeper inward and farther outward you must go to gain entry to the spirit world and pass through the gateway into memory. Time does not exist here, but all you have ever known is within the unceasing moment of the present. Move onward now from the spirit-shrine and into the memories beyond. Release your mind to give them form and substance anew, to find what you must seek with the clear and eternal vision of the soul. *Remember!*'

It seemed at first that some part of me attempted to resist him, as I felt I could not endure the sheer terror of this experience, but beyond this I knew that I simply must not fail. Then astonishingly it began to feel that something in my mind was growing strangely drowsy and calm, floating free from all my present fears, as if I drifted away like a shade into the night to approach the borders of another realm. And as these feelings grew, at last it came, like a trapped bubble rising from out of the murky depths and upward into the light: the belief that I stood once more in the nighted marshes at the outlaw's camp, bathed in the glow of their fire, while their dark and sinister shapes gathered about me. Yet now I seemed to observe all this from a place of remoteness, almost as if it were happening to someone else. Then I heard the voices of my tormentors, coarse and grating, but rising in shouts I was now clearly able to understand.

'What's he doing here? A fucking monk!'

'Looks like he's been on the beer.'

'Drunk bastard!'

They hurled me to the ground and yelled insults at me, but I knew well these were all dead men – mere ghosts in my mind – and I almost disregarded them.

' 'Ere, my lovely, 'ave something you've never 'ad before,' I heard the woman call as she grabbed at me and squatted over me. Then I crawled away while I felt a hot wetness splash onto my back. Yet throughout all this I could only marvel upon these vivid images and sensations which the shaman's remarkable powers were restoring to my memory. Now my heart shook as I recalled the deep and certain terror of my own damnation, while I saw it come: the giant shadow-thing, rising once more out of the mist as it crept into the glimmering light. And there at last I looked clearly at the form of the Fenland monster as it took shape out of the night.

It remained a thing of distortion and darkness: a towering spectral figure whose bulk seemed equally huge, its movements suggesting extreme deformity and prodigious power – and yet it possessed no apparent physical body at all, but appeared only as a mass of swirling blackness that drifted noiselessly and almost invisibly in the dark. But as it came and I gazed up into its shadowy face, I had the clear impression of hideous features twisted with insane malevolence, and then saw plainly the gleam of its eyes vividly reflected by the firelight. Now in my memory I felt myself struggle to my feet and lurch away into the dark – but this time it was into the darkness of my mind that I fled, as my nerve failed and panic gripped me, and I sought only to escape the final sight of the horror taking shape before me. But even as I turned from it, I was seized about the shoulders by what felt like fingers of iron, and I was wrenched about to look into the face of the shaman, which loomed into my view and rendered me helpless with a cold dread.

'What do you see?' his voice demanded in an icy and implacable tone. But all I saw was his face, entranced and streaked with sweat, twisted and strange. Yet most frightful of all were his eyes, or rather his lack of them, for what I witnessed there were only empty gaping sockets, twin chasms of pure blackness that seemed to blaze out at me from within the dark depths of his heathen soul. My awareness froze as I feared then that my worst doubts were true – that he had invaded my mind with some secret and sinister purpose, and now he held me spellbound and trapped like a fly in the spider's snare. 'You must tell me what you see!' his awful voice boomed and echoed inside my head. 'For I am blind in your inner world. But I may grant the gift of sight. Look deep at what is within and find strength to confront it. *Tell me what you see!*'

Now his face was fading from my view, and I felt myself thrown powerfully backwards, returned into the memory of the firelight where that massive shadow-shrouded figure towered over me. Then I felt the blood congeal in my veins, and my whole being shuddered as for a fleeting instant the vision of its face grew clear.

It was truly a monster, demonic and utterly inhuman, yet also obscenely man-like and made infinitely more hateful by the hideous mockery of its resemblance. I could never have imagined anything more bestial or horrible – so vile and uncanny in its sheer ugliness. The whole brutish countenance was covered in a sordid mass of dark straggling hair and beard, and was distorted in shape, its brows swollen by unsightly crags and bulges above the savage sunken glare of its eyes – *eyes of the darkest blue.* For as I stared at this misshapen abomination, it seemed I recognised somewhere within it a remote, debased and filthy likeness to Cynewulf himself.

The vision was gone, swept away into nothing as finally I knew the horrific truth of it. Cynewulf was not the killer – *and yet he was!* I remembered his pagan beliefs and how he had spoken of his living spirit – his dark *fetch* – his soul's rage and madness cast out and given form upon the earth. My body jolted as I broke free from the shaman's spell and looked over at the fearsome figure of Cynewulf as he sat silent and motionless, staring starkly ahead with fixed, unseeing eyes, while his fingers gripped the hilt of his sword until his knuckles grew white. I could not doubt the awful reality that his obsession was now turning into possession. As the demon rose so the man was gone. I turned to look into the sharp grey eyes of the shaman as I gasped out:

'*It is Cynewulf!* The old warrior. He is in the grip of something monstrous – his terrible nemesis. It lives again in him because in his mind it can never die. He is its pathway into our world – its earthly medium. Long ago a witch foretold it! And we are trapped here while the horror is coming. An outcast spirit… a thing of fury and malignity incarnate!'

Truly my words were not spoken to Taeppa, but were only the chaos of my thoughts given voice. I turned away from him as it seemed now I had fallen like the others into a pit of my deepest terrors, my last rational defences torn away by a crashing wave of superstitious dread I could no longer find the strength to deny or disbelieve.

Yet I clung to the wreckage of my faith. I told myself that

only the rites of the Church might serve to defeat and exorcise a malign spirit. But the man who possessed such knowledge and power was now stricken by his own terrible madness. I saw then that I must go to Cadroc and try to make him understand… but it occurred to me suddenly that his ravings had fallen silent. I moved towards him and saw him there, still kneeling inside his circle of torchlight, his body slumped forward and his head bowed in a state of apparent exhaustion and defeat, his stance like a horrible parody of religious obeisance – an act of surrender to the deepening night. Then my heart shook, for I saw what was moving towards him while he cowered and shrank before it as it rose slowly from out of the marshes like a swirling black fog – the formless thing that seemed now to have emerged from the vision in my mind and out into the living world. *It was here among us.*

'No! *Great God, no!'* Even in my terror I found the power to cry out and distract it away from Cadroc, as I heard him utter desperate sounds in a voice so thick and strained that his words were incoherent. Then I sensed the spirit's gaze fall upon me, and at once it was moving towards me, charging with silent yet tremendous speed. Wildly I turned to flee, but my muscles froze as I knew there was nowhere to escape, and I stumbled about only to see the face of Cynewulf as he stared beyond me with blank and stupefied eyes, while I looked back hopelessly to see that the horror was almost upon me. And in that instant, from inside the rushing blackness, I saw again its hideous, murderous face as it uttered a hoarse shriek and bared its great jagged teeth, and I realised then that all my wild imaginings were wrong – that in its glowering ferocity it bore no earthly resemblance to Cynewulf or to anything else that might be called human. It was a thing of insane and impossible degradation – a demon from the darkest depths.

I stood defenceless in its path. But at the final moment a figure sprang before me, and the shaman thrust out his staff as he stood to face the terror, yelling out to the others:

'Rise up! Stir yourselves! The enemy is upon us!'

From within the rippling shadow of the demon's form there materialised suddenly a giant hand, and I saw that it held a weapon like none I had ever seen: a great club with a bulbous head from which protruded long and wicked-looking spikes that were like metal talons – a terrible instrument to bludgeon and tear the flesh. The fiend lunged forward with inhuman speed, swinging down its awful weapon at Taeppa. The shaman raised his staff lengthways barely in time to counter the strike, but its sheer force sent him staggering backward as the demon followed and struck another shattering blow, and again the shaman blocked it, but this time his staff simply broke and splintered as he was thrown down onto his back, and his fearful adversary moved to close on him.

But now came another figure which sprang at the horror, and Aelfric gave a great cry as he drove his spear towards its insubstantial form, and his face was livid with a wildness and fury to match the demon's own. The fiend turned from Taeppa to meet Aelfric's attack, smiting his spear with a downward stroke of its club, driving its point to the ground and pinning it there, while it advanced and gave another guttural howl as it towered over the helpless Aelfric. Its weapon flashed upward to drive those fearsome spikes deep into Aelfric's breast, ripping open his body as blood burst from the dreadful wound, and momentarily he was lifted from his feet before he fell. The fiend tore its weapon free while it turned, standing over Aelfric's crumpled form as its baleful stare fell back upon me.

Yet now from behind us there rose the clear voice of Cadroc, splitting the night as he screeched out words of power.

'*Exorciso te, omnis spiritus immunde, in nomine Dei Patris omnipotentis...*' I looked over to see him approach, the bronze cross on his breast emblazoned by the light of the torch he carried, making him appear like a shining vision of God's wrath. He strode forward fearlessly until he stood to face the demon, and then a remarkable thing occurred. For the hideous spirit grew still and seemed to gaze transfixed upon the glowing symbol, while Cadroc screamed out Celtic curses. Yet even as he did so another remarkable thing happened. Beneath where the demon stood, the fallen and butchered form of Aelfric suddenly stirred back into life, his body resurrected as he reared up, and I saw that in his hand he clutched a small hunting knife. And there in the gloom, by the light of Cadroc's torch, I watched astounded as Aelfric's shaking hand rose to reveal that the shroud of darkness, which had seemed to be the demon's true form, was in reality a long black robe which swirled about it to cover its true frame entirely. And there was exposed beneath it a bare and hugely muscled leg which was partly covered by a skirt of animal skin, as Aelfric drove the point of his knife into the bulging flesh. The fiend gave a dreadful snarl as it staggered back, then brought down its club, smashing it with sickening force onto Aelfric's skull. But I had already glimpsed the gush of red blood which had spurted from the monster's wound. Another loud curse rose from Cadroc's lips, as with a final deadly glare the creature turned and fled, scrambling away into the night as it hobbled on its injured limb, its dark cloak fluttering about it as it went. And now it looked to me insanely like the image of a gigantic, hopping crow.

I fell to my knees beside Aelfric's corpse, gazing upon it in shock and disbelief as blood welled from the torn and steaming entrails.

'There may be time later to mourn our fallen.' A voice spoke behind me, and I looked around to see Cynewulf standing over me. His former look of defeat and despair were gone, to be replaced by one of deep and terrible rage. 'It is said that a man should not yield to grief, but instead seek vengeance. I have been shamed, made into a fool and a coward by my own fears. But I saw the sign brave Aelfric's soul most surely rose to give us. Our enemy is no dark spirit but a bestial thing of flesh and bone. So I say its evil spell is gone from me, and my soul cries out for its blood. If the monster can bleed, the monster can die! It is wounded and we must hunt it down. We finish this tonight.'

I looked at Cadroc. He too was much changed from the desperate creature I had left on the edge of the marsh. His face was now hard and determined, and I supposed he was experiencing much of Cynewulf's shame.

'Yes,' he said, his voice cold with anger. 'I too have overcome my disgrace. My time of weakness and doubt is over, and I am ready to do what God demands. I am with you.' And he drew his sword, then nodded firmly to Cynewulf.

'I have come here to join this battle,' the shaman said, as he reached down to snatch up Aelfric's spear, then began to lead the way, following along the path where the beast had fled. I paused for a moment, wondering with uncertainty whether I should go with them. I did not see how I might be useful to them, unarmed as I was. But then my eyes fell upon Aelfric's knife, lying at his side, and I picked it up and wiped away the blood. I shuddered with distress as I viewed his mangled body but reflected that perhaps his spirit now sent to me some portion of his courage. Or perhaps I did not wish to remain in that place alone. I am not certain. But I hurried off after them.

Together we raced away, hard in pursuit of our loathsome

adversary, whose true nature of being I could no longer attempt to guess. Taeppa and Cadroc went in front, and by the light of Cadroc's torch they followed the winding trail of blood.

'Tread with care!' the shaman called out to us as we left the solid ground of the island to enter into the perilous terrain of the marshes. 'There is much here that is treacherous. More dangerous even than monsters.'

Chapter Seventeen

We moved in single file, and I went at the back as we threaded a path through the high rushes, our feet sinking into the squelching ground. Suddenly I became aware that in places ahead of us there danced the macabre silvery lights of the marsh phantoms, which drew ever nearer until they shone faintly in the gloom all about us. I shivered at the sight of them and did not care to imagine what manner of sinister things they were. Taeppa slowed his pace as he attempted to steer a path away from them, but still my eyes kept returning to them as it seemed they worked their spell of dark fascination onto me. As we crept forward through a dense patch of mist the sense of a primal lurking threat filled the air and felt so intense and powerful that it was like a thing that was itself alive. But as we moved onward I realised it was only this knowledge of extreme and imminent danger that kept the shock and terror of all that we had already experienced from overtaking me.

Then we heard it, somewhere up ahead – the sudden movement of our monstrous foe as it crashed and lumbered through the vegetation on its maimed leg, and for a fleeting moment I saw its great bulk loom up in the murk nearby, before it sank down and was lost again. I knew then that we had run the wounded beast to ground, where I sensed it would be most dangerous.

'Both of you!' I heard Cynewulf whisper sharply. 'Move to my side. Our strength is in our number. We must stand together in formation. Shaman, go in the middle, with swords either side. When the beast attacks, you must engage it with your spear and try to draw it in. Yet be cautious and keep your distance. Cadroc and I will close upon it from both sides to cut it down. But seek to distract, wound and weaken rather than try to strike a fatal blow. It will be safer that way.'

I stood back as I watched them position themselves, shoulder to shoulder, as they began to advance as one, moving cautiously onward into the grey swirls of mist. We all sensed that our enemy was somewhere very close, only biding its time, as we strengthened our nerves against its inevitable onslaught. Then the rushes in front began to move and sway violently as the attack came, so swift and frightful that I feared our formation would break and scatter before its naked fury, as the beast burst upward to charge screaming at us, like an ancient thing formed from out of the mud and slime. Once more my senses reeled at the sight of it, at its sheer unearthliness, as it crouched and snarled, its demonic face contorted as drool slavered from its lips. I saw Taeppa brace himself, his spear pointed at the beast as he firmly held his ground. Then he took a step forward while his voice rose in its familiar chanting tone, calling out:

> 'Heed me, shadow walker, I command you!
> To the death-realms I condemn you,
> To the dark wastes I confine you,
> To emptiness I consign you,

To the depths I commit you,
To oblivion I compel you.
Sink back whence you came.
Let the darkness take its own!'

As he spoke these words he began to wield his spear in a series of fluid motions that seemed to weave a strange and intricate design into the very fabric of the night, his movements deft and supple as there grew about him the rising sense of an almost tangible power. The monster itself now appeared to become affected by this, as its look of raw lethality slackened into one of seeming wariness or bewilderment. Then Taeppa sprang at it, stamping his foot down hard into the soft earth as he gave a loud cry and drove out his arm, jabbing the spear forcefully into the empty air, thrusting it towards the crouching figure of the beast. The monster rose up to its full height as its terrific frame rocked and it stumbled back, and Taeppa repeated his actions while the beast growled and staggered once more, its face filled again with brutal rage, as if the awful creature were held at bay by great blows from an invisible hand.

Now emboldened, Cynewulf and Cadroc moved forward to stand on either side of the shaman, and as Cadroc advanced he raised his sword up high, assuming the stance of an avenging angel. Then he brought his arm down, smashing the sword's hilt with terrible force onto the back of the shaman's head.

Taeppa tumbled forward, falling on top of the spear and lying motionless on the ground, and for all I knew he was dead. I looked on dumbfounded as Cadroc took a sideways step, turning to face us both, pointing his blade at Cynewulf as he backed away and approached the hulking figure of the beast.

'So much for the blasphemies of wizards!' he said to us.

'Let the darkness indeed take its own. Perhaps now the odds are less to your liking?' He reached down to stand his torch upright in the mud and gazed into the eyes of the beast as he came before it, while he gripped his cross and held it in front of him. Then I could see, this time with certainty, that the very sight of the holy symbol had rendered the creature spellbound, and even as Cadroc advanced, so the beast fell back, sinking silently away into the murk and the tall reeds, to be lost from our sight in an instant.

'Back on the island,' Cadroc said as he turned to face us, 'my demon did not flee through pain or fear, but because I commanded it. We have lived together in the depths of these marshes, and you saw back in the hut that he has been lonely – so lonely – as he awaited my return, so that together we might once more be complete.' He threw back his head and gave a long sigh. 'Is he not magnificent? Are we not perfect?' At once his eyes flashed at Cynewulf, and then at me, and he gave a frown. 'I fear now we cannot let you live. You have seen that my dark angel is of living flesh, and you must not survive with this knowledge. Understand that he is sent into this world as a terrible redeemer, so men might be given faith – as it was given to me. I will pursue him and our battle will rage, and he will flee at my command to demonstrate the power of the Cross over the things of darkness. And none will ever suspect that we are truly one – the right and the left hand of God!'

As he spoke Cadroc's voice sank to a low growl from deep in his throat, his tone oddly flat and monotonous, as if he were intoning a Church ritual. Yet insanity burned like a cold flame within him. I realised now that the very sight of the monster had changed him entirely into another man from the one I had known. Two different men in one? Or one man with a damaged and divided soul?

'I must inform you,' he said to Cynewulf, who looked to be in the grip of a strange fascination as he stared back, 'that after our battle with those demons in Elmet, when we returned to seal the cave mouth, we found there, miraculously preserved among the fallen stones, a devil-child. Dark spirit transmuted and incarnated into corrupt flesh. My father brought him back with us to our hall and chained him in a dungeon, feeding him with raw meat and beating him to arouse his innate savagery, as he became an exhibit to thrill and excite the wonder of our guests. But soon his novelty faded, and his existence was almost forgotten – except by me. Because I was certain that God had given us this prodigy for a purpose. The devil-child sank into apathy in his loneliness and confinement, and would only gaze with blank, mindless eyes into the darkness of his cell. But I was his deliverance. It was I who conceived the plan to instruct and restore him, using the Cross itself as my symbol of control and chastisement. For I knew that only the power of Christ could give domination over a monster with a demonic soul. I recall the day when he looked into my eyes, and I saw there for the first time the stirrings of consciousness and reason. After that his gaze began to draw me into its depths, and slowly I grew almost lost there as our minds and wills fought for ascendency. It was at first a fearful thing to enter into this realm of darkness. But I knew that I would conquer it with God at my side. I knew in the end mastery would be mine. And meanwhile my dark angel grew to possess a size and strength far beyond that of any human child. Your story I confess made me question the truth of his infernal nature. But at last I understand exactly what he is – the child of an unholy mating between man and demon. You must see, Lord Cynewulf, that he is your own kinsman – on his human side.

'But then came the invasion of my land by the pagan armies

of King Penda. My father fell in battle, and I was forced to flee, leaving behind my country, my position and estate, and all that was rightfully mine. I was made *powerless*. I swore eternal revenge against the heathens who had dispossessed me. Yet I also saw that God had given me power and placed into my hands the perfect instrument of His retribution. My own dark angel – my shadow – *my other self!* So together we came into exile, into the remoteness of these Fens, and we learned to survive here. Now, as he grew, I began to instruct him in the art of combat – with weapons taken from my father's armoury, relics from the time of the Romans – so that our bodies might become as closely assimilated as our minds. And so we came to be one – more powerful and terrible than any man could be.'

'Brother Cadroc!' I said sharply, attempting to reach the man he had been, even while I feared that man was now swept away and irrevocably lost. 'Remember that you left this exile, to re-enter the world of men and become a monk…'

'Yes!' he said, as his voice seemed to falter and his face grew perturbed. 'I began to suffer doubts. There arose in me a voice that questioned if my plan was indeed God's will, or truly an impulse inspired by the Devil. I began to fear that by slow degrees… the darkness had gained control of me! In my uncertainty, I fled to a monastery and received the tonsure, vowing that I would remain inside while I searched my soul for the truth. But always at night I would feel him outside, his presence awaiting me in the dark, calling to me with the voice of my other self until, alone and abandoned, he began our mission to bring terror and vengeance to the unbelievers. He was crying out to me!' Now Cadroc threw back his head to unleash a dreadful roar, a blood curdling sound which rose from the visceral depths of his being as if to block out and still the warring chaos in his soul, until it seemed that the enraged spirit of the beast itself had come to inhabit and possess him. His voice grew so hoarse and growling it seemed barely human as he went on. 'But now I have come back to look once more into the face of the abyss, and at last I am convinced that it was the whisper of doubt in me which was the true voice of the Devil!'

He looked to me, and said: 'Let not your heart be troubled. My dark angel will bring death only to the pagans. Did he not spare your life? The servants of Christ he will not harm.'

It was now I saw in his raving lunacy a dreadful reflection of myself – that I had followed not the truth but only the madness. It came as a stark revelation. But I feared it was a lesson I would not live to profit by, and in despair I yelled out at him:

'The darkness has taken you utterly. You have raised up a false idol in your own image. A twisted embodiment of all your hatred. That monster is what you have come to worship. That thing of the Devil!'

'Ah!' He gave a chilling smile. 'But the Devil has his purpose, ordained by God. How might the Church prosper without him? How else might filthy heathen savages be controlled except by fear? But why do I debate with you? An outcast monk who doubts his faith. Your death will be pleasing to God's eyes.'

Now Cynewulf spoke, while he stared at Cadroc with a terrible realisation.

'My enemy is inside you!' he said. 'When my twin died… the true demon… the blind spirit of rage and vengeance in me… it passed into you!'

Suddenly he unleashed a roar of wild anger and charged at Cadroc, his sword raised ready to strike. Cadroc did not move, but only looked on coldly as the beast – his dreadful familiar spirit – sprang forward, aberrant and terrible as it burst out from the rushes and gave an awesome shriek of maniacal fury, its club meeting Cynewulf's blade. Again their weapons clashed together, Cynewulf gripping the hilt of his sword with both hands. But while he matched his opponent's blows, it was clear he could not equal its sheer strength, and its brute force was unstoppable as it drove Cynewulf back, their two giant shapes moving away into the depths of the marshes. I stumbled after them, desperate to see what was happening, but fearful that this was a battle Cynewulf could not win as I looked upon the malformed horror of the beast's face and heard the throaty grunting of its breath as it rained down sweeping blows. Cynewulf could only fall back and struggle to maintain his weakening defence while his adversary sought to pound him into exhausted submission. Cadroc was moving behind me now, holding his torch aloft to shed an eerie light through the drifting mist, his sword held ready for when he should choose to move upon me for the kill. As I stumbled before him I felt my feet sink ever further down into the soft mud, but Cadroc's advance would not allow me to stop or turn back, yet drove me relentlessly onward into the deepening mire.

But now came the end of Cynewulf's armed resistance, as I saw the beast land a final crashing blow, and Cynewulf's sword was wrenched from his grip and sent spinning away into the dark. Yet even before the beast could swing its arm back, Cynewulf sprang forward to clamp his hands about its wrist, hurling his full weight and strength against its vast frame as he strained with every sinew to keep its fearful weapon from him. The monster stood, solid and immovable, as the iron grip of its great hand closed around Cynewulf's throat. But then, as they grappled, I saw the beast's injured leg suddenly buckle, and they staggered backwards, locked together as they fell, plunging downward into a deep mud pool. The beast sank beneath Cynewulf's weight and was at once entirely submerged, while Cynewulf sank to his chest before he reached out to halt himself by grabbing at a tussock of thick grass that grew at the pool's edge. But as I gazed below him into the pit of inky blackness, I saw the mud around him begin to shift and stir, and somehow I knew what must come next. Then in a moment it burst up, that mud-soaked horror, screeching out as it broke through the bog's surface, its hands clinging to Cynewulf, climbing forward as it used his body to gain purchase, struggling against him and pushing him deeper down into the mire as it clawed and scrambled its way upward, and I knew that within moments it would fight its way free from the clutch of the morass.

At once the glimmer of torchlight grew brighter, and I looked around to see Cadroc move behind me, looking on with satisfaction as he saw the beast begin to rise up from out of the bog. Then he turned his eyes to me.

'Nowhere left to run,' he told me coldly. I stood upon the edge of the bog, and could retreat no further. So I came about to face him, holding up Aelfric's knife to point it at him. He glanced at it as he raised his sword, and his eyes met mine as his face filled with a look of scorn. And as I stared back at him my heart burned suddenly with pure anger and defiance.

Then I did something he could not have expected. I cried '*Cynewulf!*' and looked out to see that by now only the old warrior's face was still visible above the bog's surface as I threw the knife so that it slid and skittered across the mud, and as it came to rest I saw a grimy hand reach up to grasp it. Then with a bellow Cynewulf was striking out at the struggling thing above him, driving the knife's blade again and again into the body of the beast as he let go of his hold upon the bank to clasp his arm around it and drag it down. The air was filled with its terrible shrieks of pain and Cynewulf's rising roars of triumph. Within moments, they began to sink, and as they fought, they were gone, the mud rising to smother their faces and fill their gaping mouths as they were swallowed together into the devouring darkness – the last two scions of their cursed blood.

As the echoes of their cries died away, a deep silence fell. Then Cadroc began to rave and howl with demented grief and fury, and his eyes were fixed on me with venomous hate. He came at me raging, and I tripped backwards until the earth beneath me was gone, then I was submerged deep within the soft mud. As it closed around me, I helplessly watched Cadroc advance, his eyes blazing and his legs sinking into the swampy ground as he strove to reach me, and I saw that he must either kill me himself or drive me to my death farther out in the bog. But at the end I knew my life had been well spent. So I tore my arm free and pointed a finger at him as I cried out:

'A man may be what he chooses to be. But that miserable creature had no choice. You chose for it – and see what you chose! God sees you and knows you. And I curse you. May the flames of Hell take you!'

He thrust out his torch and drew back his blade to strike. Yet even as he did so there arose from the mud a great bubbling and gurgling, then the bog gave an obscene belch, and I felt it suck me downward as there came from out of its unsettled depths a reeking miasma, a great stench of rotting matter which filled the air and rippled visibly like a haze within the mist. It was so suffocating and foul that I could not breathe it in, and my head spun and sank down as my sight grew dim. And in a moment, the air around Cadroc simply burst into flame, his torch igniting into a howling blaze that was like the fires of Hell roaring up from out of the earth – or like the rising of a furious giant phantom of the marsh. Cadroc was stuck screaming in its midst, his flesh burning and shrivelling, his eyes blinded, his robe alight. I turned my face away as I felt the raging heat scorch my skin, and as it subsided I looked back to see the blaze was shrinking into ripples of blue flame that streaked and danced across the surface of the bog.

Now Cadroc toppled forward onto the mud, lying face-down before me, and I began to move steadily, grasping at him to pull myself forward and crawl over him, using his body in an effort to free myself from the deadly grip of the mire. I felt him stir weakly beneath me, and I was half free when he began to thrash and struggle, and started to sink into the depths. I was being pulled with him into the endless dark as I kicked out and lunged forward, grabbing desperately at the half solid earth and clumps of grass in front with slipping scrabbling fingers, even as I felt frantic hands claw at me from beneath to pull me down. Cadroc's body twisted as his head rose out of the swamp beside me, and I looked around into the grisly ruin of his face, blackened by mud and flame, his hair burned away and his skin hanging in blistered lumps as his withered eyes still seemed to glare at me with insane hatred. I smashed out with my fist, striking at him desperately to drive him down as he gripped me with frenzied strength to drag me with him. Exhaustion and hopelessness were overcoming me as I sank into the mud, and its blackness entombed me and felt finally inescapable as it held me suspended, beyond the power to struggle further as my strength failed and I surrendered myself to that graveyard of lost souls where lonely things of rage, despair and madness lay newly buried.

But now I grew dimly aware that somewhere far above me my fingers had clutched at something firm, and it felt like another hand had grasped mine to draw me upward.

In a moment my body was stirring back into life, slipping free from the weakening grip of the horror that clung to me below, moving up through the suffocating darkness with new determination as my head burst back into the night air, my lungs gulping as I fought tortuously to drag myself onto firmer ground.

Freed at last, I lay exhausted and unable even to think what kind of wonder had just occurred, as the full weight of all my terrors finally bore down on me. But even as I drifted towards oblivion, I looked up in the dull glimmer of Cadroc's torch, which lay fallen at the bog's edge, to see vaguely a figure standing over me. I could only suppose that it must be Taeppa, but I could not see its face or form clearly, only sense its eyes upon me as my head sank wearily to the ground. But it seemed then I knew a strange vision – that for a moment it was I who stood above myself, looking down at my own body as it emerged from out of the yawning darkness, wet and slithering and crying into the night as it gasped and struggled to draw breath. It looked to me like a thing newly born.

Once more my head jerked upwards, but now I saw no sign there of any figure. I lay quite alone. But there came the overpowering certainty that Taeppa *needed me*.

I lurched to my feet, snatching up the dying torch, and stumbled away into the mist and darkness until I came to the place where he lay. He had not moved and seemed to be dead, but then I found he was still breathing faintly. With a strength beyond any I knew remained in me, I grasped him under his arms and raised him, dragging him back onto the island where I found our bonfire still smouldering. I rebuilt it until it began to blaze again. In its light, I examined the wound on the back of Taeppa's head: a hideous gash which still gushed blood from beneath the matted tangle of his hair. There was clean water in his canteen, so I washed the blood away, but as I did so there came a deep feeling of hesitation and doubt within me, for it seemed that two sides of my being were even now locked in conflict. As I looked at Taeppa I seemed to know with a desperate sense of urgency what it was I must do, but still in some fearful part of me I held back from it. Yet beyond this there came to me a feeling of resolution and clarity, with a growing certainty that my doubts were only the echo of old beliefs which no longer served me and must in turn give way to something greater.

I took Taeppa's bone-handled knife from his belt, then thrust its blade deep into the heart of the fire. And when I drew it hot from the flames, I summoned all my strength, faith and conviction as the words of the pagan spell came from inside me, deep and clear and unfaltering:

'I entreat the great ones, keepers of the heavens,
Earth I ask, and sky; and the gods' high hall,
And the fair holy goddess, to grant this gift of healing.'

Then I laid the burning knife, again and again, onto the gaping wound, and watched in wonder as the seared flesh was knitted together to staunch the blood, while the sight of it seemed to reflect a great joining and healing of something inside me: the profound sense of a numinous power and wisdom that felt truly like the ancient spirit of all my people, reaching out to welcome me home.

Now I took Taeppa's leather bag and found inside it his jar of salve, which I applied to his wound while I recited more of the half remembered words of his charms. But the sheer intensity of all these things finally overcame me, and I must have fallen exhausted into a deep sleep.

I awoke with the dawn and looked about me in growing wonder at the silvery strands of shining mist that shone in the waking light as it gently suffused the darkness, and the Isle of the Dead appeared to become suddenly transformed and imbued with a subtle and mystical beauty which seemed astounding and unworldly to my eyes. And in those few moments I imagined something remarkable – that perhaps light and darkness were themselves things that existed as one beneath a greater reality, and the purpose of their eternal struggle was not to gain victory, but something far deeper. It was to achieve harmony, balance and growth. I turned to look out into the fog-shrouded marshes, then remembered how I had fallen deep into the pit, and stared into the face of death, and cried out that a man might be whatever he chose to be. Then my life had been saved by a miracle. It had been given back to me.

Now I looked again in Taeppa's bag and found some linen bandages inside it. As I began to bind his head, Taeppa started to stir and finally opened his eyes to look up at me.

'What has happened?' he said, as he flinched with pain.

'Be still,' I told him. 'All is well. The enemy is dead.'

'What was the enemy?' he murmured, his wits confused. 'A man or a monster?'

'A man and a monster!' I answered. 'But in truth I cannot say which one was which.'

When the mist began to clear, the island was deeply tranquil, and already it was hard to believe that in the night such horrors could have occurred there. At Taeppa's insistence I took his cloak to spread over poor Aelfric's body to leave him as decently as we could. I spoke a prayer over him, not a liturgy of the Church but words which came from my own heart. Then we set off.

Taeppa was still weak and disoriented, and badly needed rest and care. He clung to me for support as I retraced the safe path of our own tracks through the marsh from the previous day, and then onward. At last I saw the sign of smoke spiralling into the cloudy sky in the distance, and after hours of slow and wearisome progress I stumbled back into the village at Sceaf's ford, where women cried out in alarm, as the savage-looking men rushed up thrusting their knives and axes towards us. We must have been a dreadful sight, soaked in mud and blood. But in anger and exhaustion I swept out my arm at them and shouted:

'Put down your weapons! The monster is dead. But this man is injured.'

They backed away and lowered their blades as they recognised that we were indeed only men.

Taeppa was taken at once and put to bed, while I stood outside and with relief pulled off my mud-encrusted robe for the women to take and clean, while buckets of water were brought for me to bathe myself as the villagers crowded about me to hear my news. The Fenland monster was a creature controlled by a mad Christian, I told them – a terror created so the Church might then be seen to contain it. But both of them now lay buried beneath the marshes.

Soon I rested, but that evening I was brought to the village hall, where a feast had been prepared in my honour. When I entered the hall, the men rose from their benches out of respect and were not seated again until I was escorted into the chair of the high guest. Indeed it was much like the first evening I had spent on my journey into the Fens. But I was entirely a different man. That night I felt truly alive. I laughed and danced with the village women, and rejoiced among those people, and sang with them their old songs of gods and heroes and monsters.

I knew a sense of freedom and fellowship in their company that previously I could not have imagined. I drank beer until my head was spinning, and when the great joints of meat were served up, I grew suddenly aware as I smelt them that I felt more hungry than I had ever been before. I was simply ravenous. And as I gorged myself happily, I understood that I was breaking the fast which had been my whole life.

Epilogue

The dawn is almost here, and with it our companionship must end. There is little more to tell, only to say that I soon journeyed back across the Fens to the place of my hermitage. And when next Ailisa came, much concerned by my sudden departure, I took her for the first time into my arms. And when later I broke my vows, I did so gladly, knowing at last that my reconciliation with God was complete. Thus it was that I returned from my long exile to become human again – to be a man at long last. For I have looked deep into the abyss and seen there what may become of those who are cast out and driven to exclusion. So it was also that the bleak swampland which had once been the place of my penance became instead my beloved sanctuary and home. My whole world was transformed about me, for I saw it now with the true vision of the soul. Ailisa became my wife, and mother to our children, and our lives together have been blessed, for the outside world could not touch us there. You will see that I still wear the symbol of the Cross, but I wear it now upon the robe of a shaman, for I found in Taeppa a willing teacher and true friend. Since I passed through the fire, I have been the servant of no doctrine or creed save that of my own will and conscience. For the Church has given up its search for knowledge and truth in the pursuit of worldly power. It now exists principally to serve the interests and ambitions of those within it, and has become so dominant that even kings have been known to lay down their authority for the greater prize of an abbotship or bishopric. Entranced by the baubles of today, our world has cast aside the wisdom of the ages. But it may not always be so, for who can see clearly into the future? I must hope that to the enlightened men of posterity, the turmoil of these times will seem like only the petty squabbling of children. I hold fast to my faith that tomorrow will be better, and mankind will be drawn stumbling onward towards the light. For I know that light may be found in unlikely ways, and that it shines most brightly within the darkness.

Historical Note

The pagan Anglo-Saxon culture was oral, not written, so what information we possess about it comes from the works of Christian monks who were basically hostile to their subject. However, a wealth of information survives from medieval Scandinavia – and in particular Iceland – which was converted to Christianity much later than the rest of Europe, in the numerous sagas and works of men like Snorri Sturlusson, who in the 13th century had a clear sense of nostalgic affection for the traditions of the pre-Christian past.

It is not possible to provide a very accurate map of seventh-century England, given that my story is set at different times during that century, since the boundaries of the lands were constantly changing as kingdoms competed for territory and power, and smaller lands were absorbed into larger ones. The land of Elmet gives a good example of the vicissitudes of the times. At the beginning of the seventh-century Elmet occupied an area roughly equivalent to the later West Riding of Yorkshire. It was an independent Romano-British frontier state, bordered by the Anglian lands of Deira (eastern Yorkshire), Lindsey (Lincolnshire), and Mercia (the Midlands), and the Brythonic land of South Rheged (approximately Lancashire). In around 604, King Athelfrith of Bernicia (an Anglian kingdom in the North-East located between the River Tees and the Firth of Forth) invaded Deira to the south, and drove out its ruling dynasty, joining both lands into what would become the kingdom of Northumbria. A Deiran prince, Edwin (whose later and somewhat tortuous conversion to Christianity is recounted at length in Bede's *Ecclesiastical History of the English People*) was forced into exile and for years became a fugitive from the agents of Athelfrith, who sought to exterminate him as a dangerous rival. Another Deiran prince, Edwin's nephew Hereric, took refuge with the King of Elmet, Ceredig, who then betrayed and murdered him at Athelfrith's instigation.

The same tactic was employed with King Redwald of East Anglia, while he gave refuge to Edwin, to whom Athelfrith sent envoys, at first offering rich rewards to kill or surrender Edwin, but finally threatening war. Redwald vacillated, but was persuaded by his queen to support Edwin. The armies of East Anglia and Northumbria clashed at the Battle of the River Idle in 616, where Redwald was victorious and Athelfrith was slain, clearing the way for Edwin to be installed as the new king of the whole of Northumbria. The powerful alliance between Redwald and Edwin now secured for Redwald the title of *bretwalda* or 'Britain-ruler', a position of pre-eminence over the other Anglo-Saxon kings in Britain.

Edwin next invaded and annexed Elmet, expelling King Ceredig in revenge for the murder of Hereric, or perhaps using this as a pretext for his actions – if any were needed, since it marked the beginning of an aggressive policy of westward expansion into British territory, with Edwin extending his overlordship far into those lands, so that he was able to claim the status of *bretwalda* for himself upon Redwald's death. But these successes fostered animosity. In around 632 the Christian King Cadwallon of Gwynedd, war-leader of the Britons, formed an unlikely alliance with the pagan Angle, Penda of Mercia, who combined their forces to defeat and kill Edwin at the Battle of Hatfield Chase. Cadwallon went on to ravage and briefly conquer Northumbria – until he too died in battle – and Elmet presumably regained independence under British rule (at least this is what I have inferred for the purposes of the novel) until finally it was seized by Penda, then probably became as a bone between two dogs – alternately a province of Mercia and Northumbria during their continuing struggles for supremacy. Writing in the eighth-century, Bede refers simply to the Forest of Elmet.

Such was the turbulence and instability of the age. Into this toxic mix of shifting alliances between Britons and Anglo-Saxons, Celtic Christians and pagans, came the Roman Church – successor to the Roman Empire, and as an enduring symbol of Rome's past glory still the main power-broker of Western Europe – determined to extend its sphere of political influence and control, and sweep away all opposition; to conquer new territories (or re-conquer old ones) by now claiming authority over the souls rather than the bodies of its subject peoples. Paganism and Celtic Christianity were by comparison uncoordinated and localised, lacking the cohesion to stand for long against the organised assault of the Roman Church – although it might be argued that with saints to take the place of heathen gods, and the symbol of the Cross to replace the idols the Christians affected to despise, paganism was never truly abandoned but merely repackaged, retaining enough of its original content to make it palatable to heathen converts. Kings, who as pagans were little more than tribal chieftains and warlords, were no doubt often keen to convert, since to become Christian was to improve their status by adopting a faith which spoke of divinely ordained royal power (although of course, according to the word of Pope Gelasius I in the fifth century in the doctrine of the Two Swords, a king's authority was secondary to that of the Church, being merely temporal instead of spiritual) and enter a greater world of wide international connections – to start to become 'civilised' after the Roman fashion. Those who did resist were doubtless soon made to feel backward-looking and unenlightened – always a standard ploy by those determined to gain power over the minds of others.

In conclusion I must acknowledge a debt to the late Bertram Colgrave, who in his edited translation of *The Life of St. Guthlac* (Cambridge University Press 1956) first suggested the idea that Guthlac's demonic visions as a hermit in the Fens might have been as a result of hallucinations induced by lysergic acid (LSD) in the ergots which grew on his damp stale bread.